Return to Gone-Away

Also by Elizabeth Enright

GONE-AWAY LAKE

TATSINDA

ZEEE

THIMBLE SUMMER

THE FOUR STORY MISTAKE

THE SATURDAYS

SPIDERWEB FOR TWO

THEN THERE WERE FIVE

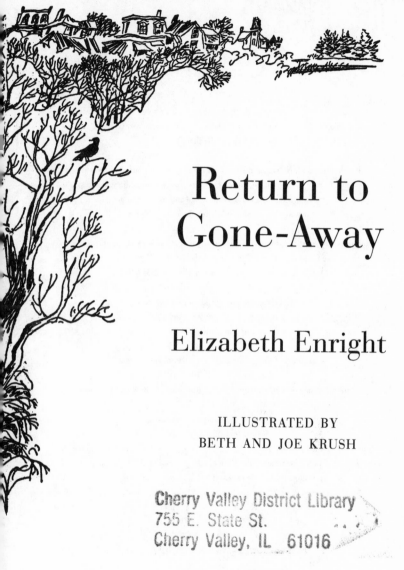

Return to
Gone-Away

Elizabeth Enright

ILLUSTRATED BY
BETH AND JOE KRUSH

AN ODYSSEY/HARCOURT YOUNG CLASSIC
HARCOURT, INC.
SAN DIEGO   NEW YORK   LONDON

First Harcourt Young Classics edition 2000
First Odyssey Classics edition 1990
First published 1961

Library of Congress Cataloging-in-Publication Data
Enright, Elizabeth, 1909–1968.
Return to Gone-Away/Elizabeth Enright; illustrated by Beth and Joe Krush.
p.   cm.
"An Odyssey/Harcourt Young Classic."
Sequel to: Gone-Away Lake.
Summary: Eleven-year-old Portia and her family return with cousin Julian to the site
they visited the previous summer, this time to take possession of a large Victorian house,
unoccupied for fifty years and full of treasures and secrets.
[1. Vacations—Fiction.   2. Cousins—Fiction.]   I. Krush, Beth, ill.
II. Krush, Joe, ill.   III. Title.
PZ7.E724Re   2000
[Fic]—dc21   99-55278
ISBN 0-15-202263-5   ISBN 0-15-202256-2 (pb)

Printed in the United States of America
C E G H F D B
E G H F D   (pb)

*For Peter Montgomery Benton
and his sister Gata*

CONTENTS

1

A Wish Come True

"You mean really? You mean honestly? Daddy, you mean you really, really, really *did?*" cried Portia Blake, hugging her father around the middle and at the same time jumping.

"You mean cross-your-heart truly?" demanded her brother Foster, grabbing his father's arm with both hands and at the same time jumping. Their dog Gulliver, a boxer, added to the general pandemonium by barking emphatically, and also, of course, jumping.

"Down, everybody, down!" protested Mr. Blake. "Your joy is too athletic; it jars my bones. Yes, I do mean really, I do mean honestly. Your mother and I signed the papers today, and the Villa Caprice is ours!"

"We'll have to think of a new name for that house right away," said Mrs. Blake.

"Ours! Ours! Ours!" yelped Portia, still jumping, but releasing her father. She was eleven-and-a-half years old; her brother Foster was seven. The thing they wished for most in all the world had just happened, and this can be an unsettling experience. Portia now launched into a sort of swooping waltz; then she stopped abruptly and said: "I dibs the round room! May I, Mother? The little round room in the turret? Please?"

"I don't see why not," her mother said satisfactorily. "Daddy and I will have the big one with the fireplace. Think of all those rooms! We could each have two apiece if we wanted." She paused, looking rather dreamy and preoccupied. "Yellow, I think," she remarked. "Yellow, or a pale, pale green."

"Yellow what?" asked Foster.

"She means curtains," said Portia, who understood her mother very well.

The Villa Caprice, which was the cause of all their rejoicing, was a large elderly house a hundred miles away in the country, not far from the heavenly spot that Portia and her cousin, Julian Jarman, had discovered the summer before. This spot was called Gone-Away Lake, and as its name implied, a live lake that had once sparkled there had long ago simply disappeared, vanished mysteriously into the earth, leaving in its place a great stretch of swamp and bog. This was fascinating for exploring purposes:

there were turtles to be found there, and curious mosses and wild orchids; there was a quaking bog that you could jump on, and another bog, a dangerous one, safely bridged now, called the Gulper, where Foster had nearly lost his life the summer before. There was the island Craneycrow, towered with evergreens and hiding a little house; but best of all, at the edge of the reedy, whispery expanse of swamp, was the settlement of fancy old ramshackle houses that the summer people had built there long, long ago when Gone-Away was a true lake. Nearly all the houses were broken and abandoned; only two people lived there now: old Mrs. Minnehaha Cheever and her distinguished brother, Mr. Pindar Payton, who had returned, after many years, to live out their lives in the place they had loved as children. They were an interesting, eccentric pair who liked and enjoyed children, and children in turn liked and enjoyed them.

The Villa Caprice, the Blakes' new possession, was set a short distance beyond Gone-Away, surrounded by woods and a tangle of vine-woven hedges. It had belonged, many years before, to a strongminded lady of wealth named Mrs. Brace-Gideon, who had perished in the San Francisco earthquake of 1906. She had left no survivors, no one had ever claimed the house, and until the summer before, when the children had crept in to explore it, nobody had entered it in more than fifty years! Everything in the house, except for the velvet shawls of dust that covered every surface, was just exactly as Mrs. Brace-Gideon had left it. Rooms and rooms to be explored! Cupboards and cupboards to look into! Hundreds of books to be examined! And all of this now belonged to the Blakes. No wonder they were overjoyed.

"Of course it's as ugly as a horned toad," said Mrs. Blake. "But so solidly built and so comfortable; and I'll simply force it to be pretty inside!"

"And think of the grounds," her husband said. "The old orchard, the fine trees—"

"Oh, I can't *wait*," cried Portia, beginning to swoop again.

"Yikes, and that suit of armor on the landing," said Foster, remembering. "When I get there, I'm going to try it on." Then he said: "But I think we should get another dog for that house; it's too big for just one. And maybe a cat? And maybe a horse, or two horses?"

"And maybe a wallaby and maybe an anteater," his father said. "First things first, Foster; wait till we move in."

"Oh, there's such an enormous amount to be *done*," moaned Mrs. Blake. "It's staggering to con-template." But though she moaned, she looked as happy as a lark; interested and alert, the way women usually look when they are thinking of fixing up a house. "Perhaps red," she said.

"Curtains?" Foster asked.

"Linoleum," replied his mother.

Mr. Blake, however, seemed suddenly rather solemn. "I wonder about the plumbing," he said thoughtfully. "Great Scott, the pipes are probably rusted through; we'll have to have all new ones. And of course there's no electricity. No phone. No refrigeration. Maybe it isn't such a bargain after all."

"Oh, Paul, we got it for a song!" said Mrs. Blake. "*Even* with the pipes, and *even* with all the cleaning and painting, and ripping off that awful porch, it will still be a bargain! And the electricity can wait. We'll do with lamps and candles for the present."

"When can we go and see it, Mother? How soon, now that it's ours?" begged Portia. "Promise not to go without us the first time, will you? Please? Please?"

"Please?" echoed Foster.

"We thought we'd all go up together during your spring vacation," their mother told them. "Aunt Hilda and Uncle Jake said they'd be glad to have us, and I know they meant it."

"And spring vacation's only two weeks off!" Foster exulted. "Oh, man! Oh, brother! Oh, hot dog!"

"Oh, I can't *wait*," groaned Portia.

But of course she had to wait, and though the days ground by deliberately like the cars of a slow freight, they were over at last, and the Blake family set out on their journey to claim their new old house.

They went by train, as they did every year (Gulliver was boarded at the vet's), but never before had they gone so early in the season. It was only the middle of March, and the trees were leafless. The winter had been severe; the country that sped by the windows looked chastened and bare, and the sky was a cold gray; crows speckled it here and there. In some of the dun-colored fields there were still old rags of snow.

"It's not what I'd call a propitious day," said Mr. Blake.

But nothing could dampen the spirits of the family. To them, train travel in itself was a kind of festivity, and to Portia and Foster, at least, food tasted better in a dining car than anywhere else in the world.

"And it certainly ought to," complained their father, frowning at the menu. "Great Scott, at these prices we should be ordering stuffed ortolans, or nightingales' tongues, or braised papyrus roots from the Nile Delta instead of ham-and-eggs and fried potatoes."

"And a club sandwich for me," Portia reminded him. When it came, she ate every single thing on the plate, including the pickle, the olive, the rather wan lettuce leaf, and left only the two frilled toothpicks that had held the sandwich together. Those Foster put in his pocket. "I can use them for something sometime, but I don't know what yet," he explained.

It was not so very long after lunch—an hour or two—before the train slowed down, coasted on for a bit, and stopped with a clatter at the Creston Station, where the Jarmans always met them.

And there they were, all of them, smiling and calling: big Uncle Jake with his big mustache, pretty Aunt Hilda hurrying forward, and Julian, their son, who was Foster's idol and Portia's best friend, even though he was her cousin and a boy besides.

There was a commotion of greetings and embraces. "Julian, you've grown a year's worth," said Mr. Blake.

Julian would soon be thirteen: a tall, skinny boy with orange-red crew-cut hair, freckles, glasses, and large eager-looking front teeth. One would not have guessed from his appearance that he was his school's best athlete, wonderfully coordinated. In addition to his skill at sports, he was of a scientific turn of mind, and an ardent amateur naturalist. It was his pursuit of an uncommon butterfly the summer before that had led him and Portia into the great swamp of Gone-Away, and indirectly to the battered resort houses where they had first made the acquaintance of Mrs. Cheever and her brother.

"How are they? Aunt Minnehaha and Uncle Pin?" was the first question Portia asked.

"They're O.K., they're fine," Julian said. "You should see Uncle Pin on ice skates! He's a wizard!"

Uncle Jake, in the lead, drew up beside a blue station wagon and opened the door.

"You have a new car!" exclaimed Portia accusingly. She had been very fond of the old one, which she had known since her babyhood.

"We had to," Uncle Jake said. "The other one got arthritis."

"*Car*-thritis, you mean," corrected Julian, who was partial to puns.

"Anyway, it's only new from our point of view, not from the dealer's," Uncle Jake said. "It was already three years old when we bought it."

The station wagon proved to be very comfortable and more spacious than the old car. A pair of ice skates, a box of dog biscuit, one mitten, and some library books lent a homely air to the interior.

"It *smells* just like the old one," Foster remarked approvingly. "I mean it smells exciting."

They drove through Creston and out into open

country; then through the village of Attica, where Uncle Jake's newspaper, *The Attica Eagle*, was published; and on again through countryside: bare, leafless, neutral-colored.

"Winter's never going to end." Portia sighed.

"I have news for you: it's ended already," Julian told her. "Tonight you'll hear the peepers, and you'll know. And down near the brook the skunk cabbages are poking out their snouts already. Those things don't just kid around; they mean *spring!*"

The road lay between woods; presently they came to a driveway marked by the Jarmans' mailbox, and they turned in.

"Almost there!" cried Foster. "I'm hungry." Feeling happy often made him hungry; he had noticed it before.

"Well, I had a sort of premonition," Aunt Hilda said. "So I made some peanut-butter cookies and a batch of brownies and an angel cake."

"Man!" said Foster, from his heart.

They rounded a bend in the drive, and there in the midst of its winter lawns was the Jarmans' pleasant house.

It was wonderful to be there again, the Blakes thought. Indoors, a fire was snapping in the living-room fireplace. The dog Katy (who was Gulliver's mother) rushed to greet them, pleasure showing in her charcoal-colored face. Othello, another of her sons, took the cue from his mother and demonstrated his enthusiasm by a volley of friendly barks. Thistle, the family cat, was another story. He came into the room with a who-cares look on his face, strolled off under the piano, skirted the bookcase, disappeared under the couch for a while, and then, only inadvertently it seemed, fetched up by Portia, rubbing his sides against her legs and beginning to purr.

"Oh, you old fraud," Portia scolded, and she picked up the big warm cat and cuddled him in her arms. "Oh, you old faker. Listen to him purr, Mother," she said. "He sounds just like the Frigidaire at home."

Foster was hopping first on one foot, then on the other, in front of Aunt Hilda. It was his peculiar way of reminding her about the cookies and brownies; more polite, he thought, than asking right out loud. It worked, too.

"Yes, of course," said Aunt Hilda, standing up. "Come along, everyone who's hungry. Refreshments in the kitchen!"

Portia, lagging behind the others, said to Julian: "Do you think it's too late to go and see them?"

"Aunt Minnehaha and Uncle Pin? No, it's still a long way off till supper. Let's just eat a little something to keep our strength up, and then we'll go."

Julian's idea of a little something to keep his strength up was as many brownies and cookies as he could put away before his mother said "No!" Portia was nearly as bad. But the process did not take very long after all, and soon, well-muffled against the raw March wind, they were trudging along the familiar route to Gone-Away.

2

Return to Gone-Away

As they came up over the ridge in the woods, they had their first glimpse of Gone-Away Lake; Portia's first glimpse since September.

"Half a year!" she exclaimed. "Jule, do you realize it's *half a year* since I've been here?"

The place looked different, too. In the great swamp the old reeds had died down; just visible among them were the new ones rising: millions of little light green spears. But Craneycrow Island appeared the same, with its somber evergreens, and across the swamp the battered resort houses with their tipsy porches and tottering turrets seemed no more damaged than they had in the fall. The strange scene, which some people might have found desolate, was to Portia and Julian the most welcome sight in the world.

"And look, there's the dear, beautiful, glorious Machine!" cried Portia.

The Machine, lofty and narrow, was an ancient Franklin automobile, far older than Portia and Julian; quite a lot older even than their parents. It had large staring headlights that gave it an expression of alarm, a roof like the roof of a carriage, and a great deal of ornamental brass, highly polished. This strange vehicle was Mr. Pindar Payton's pride and joy, and to ride in it, as it rattled and snorted and jiggled and chugged, was a most exhilarating experience, as the children knew. Now, however, it stood haughty and silent in Mr. Payton's front yard.

"And there's Uncle Pin coming out of the house!" shouted Portia, breaking into a gallop. "Uncle *Pin!* Uncle *Pin!* Here I am back again!"

She leaped like an antelope down the slope and then along the curving path that circled the swamp and at last, breathless, flung herself into Mr. Payton's outstretched arms. Behind her came Julian, rattling and clanking. He always clanked when he ran, being prudently equipped on any outing with a camera, field glasses, a collecting case (and sometimes a canteen and a lunch box), all hung around his neck on straps. "Because you never know," he said. "This might be the one time I'd see a prothonotary warbler or find a rare specimen of something or other."

When Portia kissed Mr. Payton, it was like kissing a basket because of his beard.

"Let me look at you, my dear," he said, putting his hands on her shoulders and holding her a little away, to see her better. "By Jupiter, you're a sight for sore eyes!"

"So are you, Uncle Pin," Portia said. She loved the way he looked: his blue eyes under strong black brows, his snow-white beard and mustache; his shabby but distinguished clothes, especially the broad-brimmed hat he always wore. She thought it had a dashing air.

"Well, by Jove!" Mr. Payton exclaimed. "This calls for a celebration indeed. Let us go at once to my sister's house and see what she can provide in the way of celebration material."

He led the way. Portia skipped behind him along the narrow well-known path, and Julian, clanking faintly, brought up the rear. To the right lay the broad swamp, shorn by winter of its reeds; to the left stood the old houses in their neglected yards. They were a tatterdemalion lot, with shutters hanging from hinges, front steps skewed crooked, porches sagging: the Delaney house, the Vogelhart house, the Tuckertown house (where the children had a clubroom in the attic), and all the others, including the one that had ceased even to be a house. The Castle Castle, named for the family who had built it, had collapsed years before in a bad storm and lay now in a great heap of rubble, all scrawled over with a withered vine.

"Oh, it's so beautiful here!" Portia sighed. "It's so heavenly and beautiful to be back."

At the extreme end of the raggedy row was the house Mrs. Cheever had chosen to live in, somewhat more respectable looking than the others. As they approached it, there was a sound of barking from within. Portia knew that must be Tarrigo, still another of Katy's children.

The door flew open and out came Mrs. Cheever, so delighted that she almost danced as she hurried forward on the path to meet them. Tarrigo bounced about her, barking.

"How happy I am to see you!" exclaimed the old lady, embracing Portia. "How wonderful to have you back!"

She looked as though she had stepped straight out of a much earlier era, for she wore only those clothes that had been stored in her family's house —the Big House, as they called it—when they had left it more than fifty years before. "Why buy new ones?" she had said. "The material is superior, and I never got fat, thank fortune, so everything still fits: my clothes, my mother's, my sisters'—why, I have enough to last me till I die!" For this reason Mrs. Cheever's dresses were always long and sweep-

ing, all her hats were large and queer, and her blouses had high collars made of lace, with little stiffenings of bone.

Today she wore a skirt of scarlet wool and a blouse with leg-of-mutton sleeves.

"You have no coat, Aunt Minnehaha; you'll catch cold!" Portia said.

"Nonsense. People don't catch cold when they

are happy, and I am very, very happy. Yes, indeed
I am. Silence, Tarrigo, silence!"

Tarrigo kept right on barking. He was in a cheerful frame of mind and thought the world should know
about it.

"Well, he's really just a puppy still," Mrs. Cheever
explained indulgently. "I'm sure he'll learn in time.
Silence, Tarry dear."

Tarrigo barked with renewed vigor.

"QUIET, SIR!" roared Mr. Payton in a fearful voice, and Tarrigo with a reproachful glance stopped in mid-bark and was still.

"Firmness is what is required," said Mr. Payton firmly, but as they entered Mrs. Cheever's house, Portia saw him bend to pat the dog. "No hard feelings, eh, old fellow?" Tarrigo's stump of a tail wagged in reply.

Mrs. Cheever owned a splendid parlor, heavily infested with furniture and objects, but her true living room—the one where everything took place— was her kitchen, and it was into this that she led them now. It was a spacious room with white walls, a huge grandmotherly kitchen range that cackled and purred with the fire that was in it, two comfortably cushioned rocking chairs, several other plain sitting chairs, many shining pots and pans, and a shelf holding a row of ancient dolls all neatly dressed that Mrs. Cheever had rescued from the Tuckertowns' house, Bellemere. They had belonged to her childhood friend, Baby-Belle Tuckertown, who, like Portia, had never really cared for dolls.

"They are company for me," Mrs. Cheever said. "I enjoy their little faces."

"Minnie, my dear, what have we on the premises in the way of a celebration collation?" Mr. Payton inquired, stroking his mustache, once to the right, once to the left.

"How I wish you would not call me Minnie!" his sister objected. "Though why I should still mind after more than seventy years, I do not know. Indeed I do not."

"It's the same with me." Portia sighed. "I hate being called 'Porsh,' but still they call me it. And I guess they always will."

"Well, I never shall," Mrs. Cheever assured her, and she went into the larder to see what she could provide in the way of refreshment.

In the end she returned with a bottle of cherry-mead (to which her brother was partial), a loaf of fresh bread, and a jar of blackberry jam.

"And the kettle is just on the boil," she said. "Whoever cares for tea shall have it."

Portia had a cup of cambric tea and that was all. She stared as Julian wolfed down bread and jam.

"I don't see how you do it," she remarked in some indignation. "You ate about a hundred and fifty-three cookies and brownies less than an hour ago. Why aren't you fat?"

"I never get fat," Julian said comfortably. "It all turns into gristle. Gristle and muscle. Look at that." He flexed his arm and the biceps humped up obediently.

"Then why don't you get indigestion?" Portia persisted. "You *ought* to."

"Never get indigestion," said Julian complacently. "My stomach knows who's boss."

"We were the same when we were boys," Mr. Payton said. "Tarquin Tuckertown and I. We had a griddlecake eating contest once, I recollect. I managed to eat twenty-two. But Tark, Tark *Tuckertown* ate thirty! Strange," he said, taking out his pipe to fill it. "I have never, since that day, been tempted by a griddlecake."

Mrs. Cheever thought it might be nice to change the subject. "How is Foster, the dear little chap?" she asked.

"He's worried because he isn't losing any teeth," Portia told her.

"Well, there's a new wrinkle!" said Mr. Payton, tamping down tobacco with his thumb. "People's problems differ, for a fact."

They watched the ritual of getting the pipe to start. Mr. Payton kept drawing on it, sucking in his cheeks, then putt-putting with his lips, as he held first one match flame, then another, to the bowl. At last a red glow curled and crinkled the tobacco grains. A comfortable fragrance of smoke was added to the other fragrances of the kitchen.

Julian loosened his belt one notch and sighed with satisfaction.

"Aunt Minnehaha, that was suave," he said. "Suave" was a word he had picked up during the winter. It performed the same service as his other words of approval, "keen," "neat," and "nifty," and was in frequent use.

"You ought to be able to make it to suppertime, now," Portia commented loftily.

"Listen to you; you sound about forty-five," Julian said, unperturbed and grinning.

It was cozy in the warm, well-ordered kitchen. The wind sounded like distant surf; the stove purred. Just outside the window that faced south, Mrs. Cheever had a bird-feeding stand. "Minnie's avian snack-bar," Mr. Payton called it. Birds were busy there: nuthatches shaped like little torpedoes; chickadees with black skullcaps.

"And when the cardinal comes, scarlet, with his stylish crest, I feel as if a prince had been to visit," Mrs. Cheever said.

"When are you going to see your new house?" asked Mr. Payton.

"Tomorrow morning," Portia told him. "They thought it was too late today."

"It *is* late, too," Julian said, looking at Mrs. Cheever's peaceful clock. "Come on, Porsh; we'd better get cracking."

"I shall run you home in the Machine," Mr. Payton decided.

"Oh, no, sir, that won't be necessary," Julian said. Portia had often noticed that Mr. Payton and his sister had what she called "a politening effect" on Julian. On her, too, for that matter.

"But yes it is necessary, Jule!" she cried now. "Oh, yes, please, Uncle Pin! I haven't had a ride in the Machine since last September!"

"By all means, then, by all means," said Mr. Payton, rising. "I'll just go and fetch my ulster; you two can come along with me, and then we'll be off. Do you wish to come, Min?"

"No thank you, Pin. I do not care to tear about the countryside."

(The Franklin's maximum speed was twenty miles an hour.)

They said good-bye to Mrs. Cheever and Tarrigo, and stepped outdoors. Already, because of the clouded sky, the day was darkening. The houses by the path looked gaunt and lonely; wind sounded in their gaping halls and porches, so that they reminded one of a collection of gigantic blackened seashells. It was spooky, it really was, and Portia, last in single file, kept so close to Julian that she stepped the shoe off his heel.

"Ow," Julian said. "What's the matter? Scared?"

"A little bit," Portia admitted.

"Well, you can go ahead of me, then, if you

want," Julian offered magnanimously, and Portia was glad to accept.

Mr. Payton's house did not look spooky. Though it was shabby, it was neatly mended here and there, and a tidy doormat lay on the front step. The striped cat, Fatly, was sitting in a window, looking out, and Portia, of course, had to go in and pay her respects to him. These he acknowledged gracefully by turning on his purr.

Mr. Payton draped himself in his ulster, returned the dashing hat to his head, and threw open the door.

"Avaunt, then, Philosophers," he said. (This was a name he often called them, since the club they maintained in the Tuckertowns' old attic was known officially as the Philosophers' Club.)

Outside in the gathering twilight, the Machine stood waiting proudly. Portia, from habit, climbed into the back seat, while Mr. Payton and Julian took turns winding the crank. The Machine was sometimes stubborn about starting, but today it decided to be kind, and after a cough and a snort, the motor came to life and the whole ancient automobile began shuddering and syncopating noisily. Mr. Payton and Julian leaped into the front seat, Mr. Payton gave a loud trumpet blast on the horn because he felt like it, and off they went.

Portia, jouncing about on the slippery back seat, was perfectly happy: riding high, with the wind snapping through her hair, and all the world going by in a jiggle. Nobody talked because in order to talk above the motor you had to yell, and nobody felt like yelling.

All too soon they were turning in at the Jarmans' drive and all too soon standing on the Jarmans' doorstep waving good-bye as the old Machine, a figure of skin and bones, went dancing spryly off toward Gone-Away.

"You know what I wish, Mother?" Portia said, later that evening. "I just wish we could stay here all through the spring till summertime, and never have to go back to the city or to school until the fall."

"Darling, it won't be for very long," her mother told her. "Only a few weeks, really. And we still have nine days here ahead of us, remember."

"I know," Portia said. She appreciated her mother's talent for making things look better and gave her a hug to show it.

Before she went to bed that night, Portia opened the window wide. Cold, damp air came in, bringing a smell of old, soaked leaves, of soaked earth. There was a sound of wind in branches, and another sound, too: the spangled, silver-noted calling of the peepers, the first sweet, jingling bell notes of the spring.

3

The House

The first one up, next morning, was Foster Blake. He had slept industriously for eleven hours and woke up all of a piece without any lingering or yawning.

In his blue-striped pajamas he swung himself down from the top deck of the double-decker bed —he refused to sleep in the lower one—went over to the door and listened. Not a sound. It must be very early, he thought. His hair from having been slept on hard was all pressed up in a one-sided crest, and his cheek on that side was redder than the other. Opening the door, he leaned out into the hall and listened some more. All he could hear was the thump, thump of a dog scratching.

Foster liked to be the first one up. It made him feel he knew something about the day that no one else did. He got dressed quickly and quietly, all except his shoes, and ignoring the thought of his toothbrush, tiptoed along the hall and down the stairs. Katy and Othello got up to greet him, snuffling quietly and wagging. They were warm from their sleep.

"Come on, you guys, I'll let you out," Foster told them in a loud whisper. He unlocked the front door and opened it. The smell of a cold morning came in; Katy and Othello raced out and Thistle entered, looking irritated.

The dogs went tearing about the lawn. Foster watched them for a minute, but it was chilly; his breathing made smoke in the air. He closed the door and tiptoed to the kitchen; he had decided to have a little practice breakfast before his real breakfast.

The kitchen was clean and quiet; the clock ticked. Thistle, drinking from his water dish, made a little slipping sound. Foster knew where everything was: the box of cornflakes, the brown sugar, and the milk. He had made a satisfactory arrangement of these things in a bowl and was eating his way through it when something darkened the window above the kitchen table. Looking up, Foster dropped his spoon with a splatter, and the sound that came out of him was a squeak. What he saw in the window was the face of a monster: green, wrinkled, with dreadful fangs and a ghastly scowl! For an instant he stared in perfect horror.

"Hi, Foss," called the monster in a friendly voice.

Only then did Foster notice the pink and in-
nocent protruding ears and the upstanding cowlick
of his good friend David Gayson.

"Hi," he called back, chagrined at having been
so taken in. He went to the kitchen door, unlocked
and opened it. Davey came up the back steps wearing his own face. The rubber mask dangled under
his chin like a hideous bib.

"Who did you think you were scaring?" Foster
greeted him pleasantly.

"You, man," said Davey. "I saw you drop the
spoon and slop the milk all over. I scared *you*.
How've you been?"

"O.K. You didn't scare me. You just surprised
me." Curiosity got the better of Foster. "But how
did you get up so high? You're not tall enough to
reach the window."

"There's a good old garbage pail. Two good old
garbage pails. I climbed up on one, *quiet* as
anything—"

"How'd you know I was in here?"

"I saw you let the dogs out when I was coming,
and I thought I'd scare you. I knew you'd probably
be in the kitchen. Could I have some cornflakes,
too? No one's up at my house."

"No one's up here, either. Sure," Foster said,
and went to find another bowl and spoon.

They sat eating and chattering, happy to resume

2 7

their friendship. From time to time Davey would extract from his pocket some object he had brought to show Foster; first it was a compass, then a cap-pistol, then a small flashlight.

"Christmas stuff," he said. "Stocking stuff."

Next he brought out a pillbox with an elastic band around it. This he opened with tender care; inside, on a nest of cotton, lay his two front teeth.

"Those are worth fifty cents," he told Foster. "A quarter apiece, man! They're my first ones; that's why. I'll only get a dime for the others. You lost any yet?"

Foster felt humiliated by his teeth.

"Not exactly *lost* them," he admitted. "But they're so loose, I can kind of wave them with my tongue."

"I got new ones coming in already," Davey boasted, stretching his mouth so Foster could have the experience of viewing two tiny scallopings of white just showing at the gum.

Foster felt betrayed not only by his teeth but also by his pockets: they were entirely empty because he had put on the newly laundered jeans his mother had laid out for him. By evening, though, he knew those pockets would have tenants.

The next things Davey produced were a sort of lariat made of rubber bands, a long chain made of paper clips, a penny that had been run over by a train, a paper puncher, and last of all, carefully folded, a drawing, which he spread out on the table. It was large and brightly colored. "How's that for a moon rocket!" demanded Davey with pride. "I drew it in school."

"Wow," Foster said politely. Actually he did not think much of it and was certain he had often drawn better ones himself. But he had not seen his friend in a long time.

There began to be sounds of people stirring overhead. The two boys looked up.

"Soon it will be breakfast," Foster said. "And after breakfast, you know what? We're going to go and see the house we bought. We bought a house, Dave, you know that? It's the old one you saw with the suit of armor in it!"

"Oh, I know *that*," Davey said. "Your aunt told me. She told me about a hundred years ago already."

So far it had definitely been Davey's morning.

The breakfast, which Davey was quite easily persuaded to share and which both little boys ate with appetites that had hardly been dimmed by the practice breakfast, was magnificent: fresh orange juice, hot buckwheat cakes with butter and apple jelly, and bacon. Aunt Hilda's breakfasts were famous: varied and original, not just an ordinary plodding through of cereal and eggs and toast.

Everyone ate a lot. Mr. Blake groaned. "Great

Scott, Hilda, a few more breakfasts like this and I'll begin to waddle!"

"Never mind, Paul," Uncle Jake told him. "We need our strength; we have men's work cut out for us. The Lord knows how long it will take to get that back door open. We never did get the front one open, if you recall."

"Hurry, everyone, to work, to work!" Aunt Hilda cried. "As soon as the chores are done, we'll all set out for the Villa Caprice!"

"We *must* get a new name for that house," said Mrs. Blake.

Upstairs, Portia made her bed with lightning speed and then, perched precariously on the ladder of the double-decker, made Foster's still more swiftly. "It looks like a relief map," she admitted to Julian, who had come looking for her. "All mountain ranges."

"The kid won't know the difference," Julian assured her. "You know perfectly well he'd sleep like a log if the mattress was stuffed with potatoes. Come on, Porsh; I want to show you how my plant eats hamburger."

Portia leaped down with a thud.

"How your what eats *what?*" she demanded, unable to believe her ears.

"My plant. It's a Venus's-flytrap. I sent away for it. It eats flies when it can get them, but there aren't any in winter, so I feed it little crumbs of hamburger."

Julian's room was a sight to behold: a museum of sorts, for Julian was a collector. He collected everything from stones to snakeskins; from fossils to butterflies; from cocoons to birds' nests. The walls were encrusted with his findings; the shelves were burdened with them. It was a fascinating place, but no one could have called it tidy.

On the windowsill, between a terrarium and a tank containing a live crawfish, was the curious plant. Each of its broad leaves was tipped with a pair of flat rosy discs like a pair of queer little clam shells, fringed with crimson whiskers.

"Now watch this," Julian said. He lifted a speck of hamburger from the saucer he held and dropped it expertly into the center of a pair of gaping shells, which closed instantly, locking the fringes together.

"Oh, let me feed one, Jule, please!" Portia begged.

There was only time for one, because now Uncle Jake was calling them and they were eager to go. It took a while to get started since Foster and Davey had chosen this moment to disappear, and no one thought of looking in the cellar. Finally the repeated shouting of their own names reached the boys' attention and brought them clattering up the wooden stairs. Next Uncle Jake couldn't find the car keys, and *those* had to be hunted for. In the end they turned up, for a reason no one could fathom, on the top shelf of the medicine cabinet. Then the telephone rang and it was a lady who wanted to talk (and talk and talk) to Aunt Hilda. But at last, at last, they were on their way, all eight of them, because of course Davey went, too.

They drove as far as Gone-Away, where they stopped for a moment to chat with Mrs. Cheever and Mr. Payton; then they went the rest of the way on foot, for the road leading to Mrs. Brace-Gideon's old driveway had long been taken over by the woods.

The day, no better than the day before, was gray and chill, and as they passed between the large stone gateposts of the drive, it was suddenly very quiet. There was no wind, and the trees, draped in great snarled capes of honeysuckle, seemed to have muffled out the noises of the world. Silence had fallen on the party, as well. It was too much for Foster. He suddenly felt called upon to give his ear-splitting rendition of an Indian war whoop. Davey attempted to outdo him; the noise startled two crows out of a tree and sent them squawking into the air. The spell of silence was shattered, and everyone began to talk again.

All of them were wearing old clothes, because, as Aunt Hilda said, "There's no sense in dressing up to cope with fifty years of dust."

Uncle Jake was carrying a toolbox. Mr. Blake was carrying a small stepladder and a crowbar. Julian had two buckets and a mop, while the women and Portia were armed with brooms, brushes, and dustcloths and had their heads tied up in bandannas.

"We look like some higgledy-piggledy leftover army," Portia said.

Walking briskly, they came to a turn in the drive, the trees thinned out, and there before them stood the Villa Caprice.

There it stood among its dead and brambled lawns, with all its windows boarded up and a big, tough, tangled vine, leafless now, tied round and round the battlements, the turrets, and the gables like a giant's wrapping twine. Beyond the house the ragged hedges looked black, and the queer tree that was called a monkey-puzzle tree looked black, too, and bristling. The whole scene was shabby and forbidding.

"Oh, *dear!*" wailed Mrs. Blake. "I didn't remember it as being quite so—quite so—"

"Bleak," Mr. Blake supplied. "And this is what we called a bargain! We must have been out of our minds!"

Aunt Hilda, who wanted to be comforting, said: "You know, I think when you've got rid of that ghastly porch and ripped the boards off the windows, you'll feel very different about it."

But though she tried, she didn't really sound convinced, and Uncle Jake was seen to shake his head.

"The place looks like a training school for witches," Mr. Blake remarked in utmost gloom.

The children, however, refused to be disappointed and went running toward the house with briers snatching at their jeans and Julian clattering more than usual because of the buckets.

"I think it's suave," he assured Portia, as he jolted along beside her. "All it needs is fixing up. Heck, it hasn't been fixed *up* in fifty years! What do they expect?"

"I don't know," Portia said, feeling grateful to her cousin and indignant with her other relatives. "I think it's a perfectly wonderful house!"

"So do I," agreed Foster, dog-trotting behind them, slightly out of breath. "It's so nice and fancy; that's what I like about it. It's got so much stuff. I think it's suave."

Portia turned to beam at him. "And you know what you are? You're a wonderful *boy*," she told him.

"Big deal," Foster said, embarrassed.

They slowed down, for they were near the house. It towered above them, very large and quiet, very old. The great porch that ran halfway around it was

supported by pillars set with cobblestones that reminded one of monstrous chunks of peanut brittle.
The unpruned vine hung down in portieres from the
eaves of the porch, and on its rotting floor were
drifts of leaves. It was a dark, unfriendly thing, and
even Portia thought she would not miss it when they
took it away.

"But what will happen to the owls that used to
nest here?" she asked.

"Oh, they'll find another site," Julian said. "If
there's one thing you don't have to worry about, it's
owls."

The slow grownups caught up with them at last,
armed with their peaceable weapons.

"We'll try the back door first," Mr. Blake announced. "The front one might as well be turned to
stone. We may have to blast!"

"Why can't we just climb in the window, the
way we did last year?" Foster wanted to know. He
would have preferred this course.

"It's boarded up again, too, remember? And
anyway we can't just go flitting in and out of odd
openings all the time like—like swallows," his father said. "We need a door. Like people."

He led the way, and they all trooped around one
corner, then another, to the back stoop, with its
boarded-up back door.

"Nailed fast, of course, and the nails are rusted," Uncle Jake said. "Well, let's have a go at it."

It took a while. Foster and Davey grew bored and began to roughhouse, tumbling on the dead grass. The women poked about the shrubbery trying to identify the bushes and decide which ones were still alive. Portia sat on one of the buckets, turned upside down, watching and whistling between her teeth; trying to, anyway; her tooth braces made it nearly impossible.

Her father and uncle and cousin worked and worked at the barricade, and finally, as they pried them loose with a crowbar, the nailed boards were wrenched free, with loud, protesting snarls.

The door they had hidden all these years was painted dark green; just an old ordinary door with a brown china doorknob, but Portia jumped up to have a look at it, and everyone else came running.

Uncle Jake waggled the knob uselessly and gave the door a kick or two.

"Locked, of course," he said. "But not bolted inside, I trust. Even Mrs. Brace-Gideon couldn't depart from a house leaving every door bolted *inside*."

"Maybe she departed from a window the way we did," Foster suggested, but no one listened to him.

Uncle Jake brought a jumble of keys from his pocket.

"From Gone-Away: old keys from other old locks," he explained. "Uncle Pin's idea. He thought that one might fit."

One did, too. Almost the very first one. It turned nicely in the keyhole, and they could hear the lock give way, but the green door, set in its ways after half a century asleep, absolutely refused to budge.

Mr. Blake sighed heavily.

"You know, you don't just *buy* this house," he said. "No. You have to go to war with it, you have to conquer it! All right, Jake, let's go."

The two big men put their shoulders to the door and gave a tremendous shove, as Mr. Blake turned the knob. The first try didn't work, nor did the second, but on the third the door burst open, and they almost fell in. The others crowded close on their heels, Foster and Davey burrowing under arms and elbows like a pair of beagles.

A cloud of dust fumed up from the floor. As it cleared, they found themselves coughing and sneezing in a dim passageway.

"I suppose this—" Mrs. Blake was starting to say when all at once Uncle Jake, who was ahead, gave a mighty yell and a leap backward.

"Great Scott!" shouted Mr. Blake at the same

instant, and Foster, whimpering, turned to scramble for his mother.

"There's somebody there! A ghost, a ghost!"

Most of them, shocked, had caught a glimpse of it: a figure standing in the passage, standing very still, as though it had been waiting for them.

4

The Victors

"Well, this is ridiculous; there can't possibly be anybody there," Uncle Jake said, looking both annoyed and sheepish.

"We must be suffering from battle fatigue," Mr. Blake agreed. "Let's solve this thing right now!" And he whipped out a flashlight.

The two men strode purposefully through the doorway. Julian followed, looking rather more tentative than purposeful.

"Oh, Paul, be careful," quavered Mrs. Blake, and Aunt Hilda, who was her sister, quavered: "Jake, don't do anything rash!"

But they had hardly time to say the words before they heard a boom of laughter. Uncle Jake stuck his head out.

"Come in, all of you, and see the watchdog Mrs. Brace-Gideon left to guard the door she couldn't bolt!"

Somehow or other Portia managed to be first, and she couldn't help gasping at the sight before her: the appalling figure dressed in black. It stood there glaring at her, with eyes that had a reddish shine, and in its black-gloved hands it held a placard printed with the words: KEEP OUT!

Of course the thing wasn't real, Portia realized, just some sort of rigged-up trick, but it wasn't very friendly, either, and she was thankful she had not come upon it by herself.

"Heavens, I'm glad I didn't run into this character when I was alone!" her mother said, echoing her thoughts.

On closer inspection the fearsome creature turned out to be built on a dressmaker's dummy.

"Modeled along the noble lines of Mrs. B.-G. herself," Uncle Jake surmised, and gave the thing a friendly spank.

It was dressed in a man's cape-sleeved long black overcoat, riddled with moth holes and furred with dust. Its head was a stuffed stocking top on which a gruesome face had been devised: eyes made of red-glass buttons behind a pair of pinned-on spectacles; a guardsman's mustache cut out of felt; and a dreadful mouth in which white beads were stitched to look like teeth. On its head it wore a Tyrolean fedora tipped a bit to one side. This and the mustache gave it an aristocratic, though shabby, appearance.

"Baron Bloodshed fallen on hard times," Mr. Blake observed.

(Always after that they called the creature Baron Bloodshed, and they were so delighted with him that later, instead of throwing him away, they moth-proofed him and put him in the attic, where he went on scaring people for years, since they kept forgetting he was there.)

"Look, he's even got feet," Foster said; and sure enough, peeping out beneath the long overcoat, there was a pair of dried-up button boots. Foster picked one up to have a look but dropped it when he saw the mouse's nest inside.

"Yikes! I don't think they're living in it, though."

Portia dipped a cautious hand into one of Baron Bloodshed's pockets and was rewarded by finding a small rusted buttonhook. She dipped into another and found an Indian-head penny, dated 1883, which she decided to keep for luck, kindly offering the buttonhook to Foster.

"All right; I don't know what it's for, though," Foster said. "But come *on;* everybody's gone ahead."

Training their flashlights forward, they started after the others: through a dark laundry, thronged with tubs and laced with clotheslines overhead;

through the dark kitchen with its dimmed old pots and pans hanging from hooks and its big rusted range under an iron canopy. Portia noted the old-fashioned coffee grinder fastened to the wall, the name of the stove, which was "The Marchioness," a tattered calendar for the year 1905. Foster noted a small window into the pantry, just the right size for him to go in and out by quietly and conveniently. Then they pushed open the screechy swinging door and went into the dining room, moving through it rather quickly, for in the darkness it looked gloomy, furnished heavily as it was with carved oak and having walls that were cordially adorned with crossed swords, crossed halberds, crossed battle-axes, and crossed spears. Foster thought that he might enjoy these; but later. Not now.

They followed the sound of voices through the front hall, where on the newel post of the broad stairway a bronze lady four feet tall stood on one tiptoe foot, flourishing a gas lamp over her head. And then they turned left into the large, elaborate room that Mrs. Brace-Gideon had always called her "drawing room."

Everyone was there, twinkling about with flashlights.

Portia and Foster had only seen the room once before, and they had forgotten how big it was and how crowded with furniture. There was a huge piano, red and gold, with stout carved ladies holding up the keyboard. Near it stood a shrouded harp, and above that, hanging from the middle of the ceiling, was a great bag like a wasp's nest, and they knew there was a chandelier inside it.

"Paul, let's get some daylight in the place," Uncle Jake said. "Then we'll know what we've got here."

The men went out the way they had come, and presently, after a noise of wrenching and banging, one window opened its eye and the daylight came in; then another and another.

"Good heavens, look at the dust!" said Mrs. Blake.

"Look at the cobwebs," said Foster.

"Look at the mildew," said Aunt Hilda.

"Look at the stuffing coming out of the chairs," said Portia.

"Oh, dear," said Mrs. Blake.

The place really was a spectacle of decay. At one end of the large room a curtain made of bamboo beads hung sadly, many of its strands fallen to the floor in little heaps; and in one corner a deep divan piled with cushions was tented over with a canopy draped on a pair of spears, and simply sagging with a weight of dust.

"A Turkish cozy corner!" Aunt Hilda sighed with pleasure. "Great-Aunt Ida had one exactly like it. I'm sure there's not another left in all the world."

"This one won't be left for very long, either," Mrs. Blake assured her. "Foster, *don't sit down on it!*"

"Heck, why not?"

"It's probably full of spiders," Portia told him.

"Or maybe rats?" Foster suggested hopefully.

His mother looked far from happy.

Aunt Hilda went over to one of the windows and, after a short struggle, managed to open it wide. The first fresh air in more than fifty years came into the room, chilly, but it brought a smell of spring. Beside the window, heavy curtains of torn damask flapped softly, shaking down more dust.

Julian came into the room carrying a stepladder that he'd found in the laundry.

"What are you going to do, Jule?" asked Portia.

"I want to set the chandelier free," he said, opening the ladder and ascending. "Hold onto it, will you, Porsh? I don't know how strong it is."

Standing on tiptoe, he began to unfasten the dark baize cover of the chandelier; dust smoked up from it; dead moths, dead spiders, dead gnats showered down.

"Ow, watch it, Jule!" protested Portia, spitting out dried moth wings.

"You're all right; you've got your head tied up in a rag. All you have to do is keep your mouth closed, but I can hardly breathe," Julian said, and sneezed six times, as if to prove his point.

"Look out below!" he called in a moment, and Portia skipped aside as the baize bag dropped to the floor in a cloudy heap.

"Wow! Look at that!" shouted Foster. "It's like an upside-down fountain!"

And that was the way the chandelier did look. Elaborate, sparkling, it had been closed away from dust all these years, and its many lusters trembled, fresh and bright as drops of ice water.

"What a lovely thing!" cried Aunt Hilda. "Barbara, do you realize what you have? A Waterford chandelier!"

"Waterford? Really? Yes, I do believe it is!" Mrs. Blake's face, which had been rather worried and upset, began at once to have another look.

Foster jumped up and down as hard as he could to see if he could make the chandelier tinkle, and he did: it even *sounded* like ice water, or like the pieces of ice in ice water.

"Foster, for pity's sake, stop!" said his mother. "Julian, as long as you've brought the ladder, would you mind taking down those dreary curtains? And now let's start our housecleaning."

Soon they were all at work; even Foster had a

cloth, which he flapped and whacked at everything, stirring up much more dust than he disposed of.

"It's fun to sweep and clean when there's plenty of *real dirt*," Portia said enthusiastically, wielding her broom. "The trouble is there's not usually enough to make anything look any better when you're through."

Outdoors the men still banged and hammered at the window boards, with Davey supervising. Indoors there was a commotion of sweeping and sneezing. The gloomy curtains dropped from their rods, pair by pair, and each time the room grew lighter. Already it seemed a different place.

Somewhere outside a bird began to sing: a real bird, not a sparrow, not a jay; and then, as if the whistling song had been a signal, the sun came out.

"Mrs. Blake, Mrs. Blake!" shouted Davey Gayson, thrusting his head in at the open window. "There's flowers out already, about a hundred of them or a million! I brought you some. Look!" He held out a handful of crocuses: small lighted cups of white and lavender and yellow. "They're all *over!*" he said triumphantly, feeling as if he had invented them.

Mrs. Blake took the little bunch of flowers. The bird sang. The chandelier chimed softly as air moved in the room, and then the sunlight caught it and all the many lusters blazed and dazzled.

"Oh, I think we're going to *love* this house," said Mrs. Blake.

"Going to? I love it already," Foster declared.

"So do I, I'm crazy about it," Portia agreed, giving her brother a hug before he could defend himself.

As for Julian, he felt so fine that he went over to the piano and played a chord that sounded like a broken bedspring.

"Perhaps someday we can afford to buy that piano a new set of insides," Mrs. Blake said, dusting off one of the stout gilded ladies that held up the keyboard. "But until then it's just going to stay here as it is; I could never bear to part with it."

"Oh, never!" Aunt Hilda agreed. "Just looking at it makes you think of all those big, fat, glorious singers that Great-Aunt Ida used to talk about: Schumann-Heink and Nordica and Nellie Melba. And of boxes at the opera stuffed with people named Vanderbilt and Astor, all flaming with diamonds and waving fans made of feathers . . ."

"It doesn't look as if it should make piano noises," Julian said. "I mean, it's so fancy and gaudy, it ought to make kind of a loud racket of tunes like a jukebox or a steam calliope."

"Or a fire engine," added Foster, influenced by the combination of red and gold; and having uttered the words, he became a fire engine himself, howling and wailing like a siren and careening busily about the crowded room, taking each corner on two wheels.

"Out, Foster, out! Out!" commanded his mother, flapping her dustcloth at him. "Go find Davey and stay outdoors!"

Willingly the fire engine departed through a window, siren going full blast.

By noon the room was beginning to show signs of being conquered. The moth-eaten rugs had been flung out of the window; so had the curtains, and so had the doleful swags above the Turkish cozy corner.

"But, Mother, please leave the bamboo curtain, will you? Please?" Portia pleaded. "Listen to the sound it makes." She ran her fingers across the strands, which did make a delicious sound: small hailstones rattling on dry leaves.

"Well, I don't know. It is rather pretty. All right, I will," her mother said. "But on one condition, dear: that you will string the beads and put the fallen strands back up again."

Portia agreed willingly to this (and lived to regret it later, for it proved to be a most tedious job and took hours. Still it looked very pretty in the end).

A sound of noon whistles, one from Attica, one

from Pork Ferry, came through the open windows, and then a welcome call from the men. They had brought the lunch from the station wagon, and everyone was starved. They all went out by way of the window, and Davey led them to the place where the crocuses, "a hundred of them, or a million," were starred over a gentle slope that once had been a lawn.

"Is the water running in the pipes yet?" Foster wanted to know, and when his father told him it wasn't, he said: "Hooray, then we can't wash, we can't wash, we can't wash!"

"Yippee!" was Davey's comment, but Aunt Hilda said: "Not so fast"; and she produced a gallon Thermos jug. "Hot water for washing hands *only*; we can't waste it on faces. And here's a bar of soap."

"Heck," said Foster, but he did the job.

Then all of them, with clean hands and dirty faces, settled down to the delightful occupation of eating sandwiches and deviled eggs and fruit and Aunt Hilda's angel cake. The sun was warm on their heads, and the air smelled of spring, and they kept looking up proudly at the queer old towered house that they were bringing back to life again.

All they were able to do that day was to clean the drawing room and the front hall. By the time they were done, the walls had been cleared of hanging wallpaper strips and dusted down; the floors had been swept, scrubbed, and waxed. The divan of the Turkish cozy corner, gingerly dismantled (and proved to be the archaeological site for many civilizations past and present of clothes moths, silverfish, spiders, and beetles), had been thrust out the window, since the front door refused to budge, to join the other discards on the grass.

Mrs. Blake kept wandering about the room and pausing to observe it, first from one angle, then another. She looked very happy and dirty. All of them were dirty, black as sweeps and exhausted, but all felt sustained by the satisfaction of accomplishment.

"Time to call it a day," Mr. Blake said at last, peering in at the window. "We've liberated thirty-seven windows and the back door. And that's enough!"

He also admired the work of those who had stayed indoors, and climbed over the sill to exclaim about the drawing room. So did Uncle Jake.

Portia and Julian were sent in search of the little boys, who were finally located in the greenhouse, resting among ancient flowerpots. They had had an extremely busy afternoon exploring what Foster grandly called "The Property."

"We found a brook way back in the woods," he

said. "We own the piece of it that goes through 'The Property,' don't we, Daddy?"

"It's ours to use, at least."

"There's a bridge across it," Davey added. "Kind of a. It's pretty rotten, I guess."

"He fell through," Foster said casually.

"Oh, Davey," cried Mrs. Blake. "Are you soaked? What will your mother say!"

"I dried off all right; it was a good long time ago," Davey assured her. "So *she* won't care."

"Well, I just hope you don't catch cold!"

All of them, in straggling procession, trailed along the nearly obliterated drive. Mr. Blake had a swollen thumb from banging it with a hammer; Uncle Jake had a crick in his back. Mrs. Blake had a bruise on her shinbone, and Aunt Hilda had one on her elbow. Julian had a cut on his hand, and Portia had a splinter under her fingernail. As for the little boys, their jeans were stuck with last year's burs; old goldenrod fuzz clung to their sweaters; and where the brambles had managed to reach their skin, they were scratched.

"We look more like a leftover army than ever," Mr. Blake observed. "But I'm not quite sure whether we're the victors or the vanquished."

"Why, we're the victors, Daddy. You *know* that!" Portia chided him.

"I wish all battles were as pleasant," her mother said. Then she said: "I don't think yellow after all. No. Something warmer. Coral or rose; or a rose pattern."

"Linoleum?" Foster asked.

"Curtains," replied his mother.

That night before he went to bed Foster emptied the pockets of his jeans, which, if they had been clean in the morning, now looked very tired and dirty, just the way he liked them.

The pockets yielded a good assortment: a brass ring from a portiere, several flaky pieces of mica, two rather bashed-in oak galls, a pinecone, a bone of unknown origin, an empty milkweed pod, and Baron Bloodshed's buttonhook.

He set the oak galls, the pinecone, and the milkweed pod on his bureau to decorate it, but put everything else back in his pockets. Pockets, after all, are to keep things in.

5

The Sheep-Lady's Secret

The next eight days flew by for the Blake family. Every morning they returned to the Villa Caprice ("I wish I could think of another name for the place!" Mrs. Blake kept saying), and every day they worked like beavers. Nor were they alone. Julian and Aunt Hilda always came with them; Uncle Jake when he could steal the time. Mrs. Cheever lent a willing hand, and so did her brother; and then there were the newcomers, newcomers who soon became friends: Mr. Lance de Lacey, the plumber, and his assistant, Henry Bayles; Mr. Matt Caduggan, the carpenter, and *his* assistant, Joe Baskerville; Mr. Ormond Horton, the painter; and old Eli Scaynes, who did not care to be called "mister" and who was going to "do something about the grounds."

The children liked Mr. Caduggan the best because he brought his dog to work. It was a large tan animal with one game leg and a bent ear, and its name was Popeye.

"Only dog in the world likes spinach," Mr. Caduggan explained. "That's why we call him Popeye. Used to be his name was Duke, but one day while I was to the phone at dinnertime, he come up to the table while my wife wasn't looking, raised up on his hind legs, and et up all the spinach in the dish. *Left* the liverwurst that was right there, *left* the ham baloney. Just et up the spinach. So we call him Popeye."

All the men were nice, however. Mr. de Lacey had a beautiful singing voice and the word "Mother" tattooed on his arm in red and blue ink. Henry Bayles handed out free chewing gum. Joe Baskerville was good at cracking jokes. Mr. Ormond Horton had a cat at home that was going to have kittens, and he promised one to Portia. Eli Scaynes knew the name of every bush, bird, flower, and tree, and was a very practiced talker.

The house that had been locked in silence for so many years rang now with sounds of calling and talking, and occasionally of groaning, as Mr. Blake received the news from Mr. de Lacey that he would "have to have all new copper piping," and from Mr. Caduggan that "the carrying timbers under the main floor is settling so bad they'll all have to be propped up on lolly-columns."

There were all the other busy sounds of banging and thumping and sawing and scraping. The ancient smell of mildew and neglect was replaced by robust smells of soap and polish; later there would be a strong odor of wet paint.

Nearly every day somebody discovered something new and important.

Mrs. Blake discovered a Lowestoft tea set wrapped up in very old newspapers at the back of a cupboard. It was white with a pattern of green ivy leaves.

"Why, I remember hearing about that tea set," Mrs. Cheever told her. "Mrs. Brace-Gideon never cared much for it; she thought it too plain. The one she preferred was a fancy one, all curlicues and gold and roses, but she knew that this one was valuable, so she kept it, thank fortune."

"Thank fortune," echoed Mrs. Blake fervently.

Mr. Blake discovered the cellar. "A full cellar!" he exulted. "Someday we can have a furnace and spend the Christmas holidays here."

"Or just plain live here all the time," said Foster.

Portia discovered a closet full of Mrs. Brace-Gideon's old party dresses: bowed and beaded and bugled and spangled and fringed; draped with festoons of ribbons and lace, and each one weighing pounds. "When Lucy Lapham gets here, we can dress up every day," she said.

Foster discovered the dumbwaiter.

In the pantry, which, planning for the future, he had entered several times already by the small serving window, he had noticed in a casual way that there was a door set into the wall. It was a square door, a cupboard door he supposed, set about three feet above the floor. One day he gave it a whack by accident, and hearing that the whack made an unusually hollow drumlike sound, he decided to open the door. It was hard work to get it open because it was stuck in its frame. (Everything in the house was stuck, being swollen with damp and disuse, and all the Blakes developed good muscles and bad blisters that summer simply from the amount of lifting, yanking, shoving, pushing, and pulling that was required of them.)

Finally, though, Foster managed to wrench the thing open, and looked in at what appeared to be a very small elevator in a shaft.

"Hey, Dave!" yelled Foster. "Come look at this!"

Davey came from the kitchen, where he had been industriously grinding up acorns in the coffee grinder; a fact unknown to Mrs. Blake.

"What is it?" he inquired. "An elevator?"

"Not for people. Maybe for dogs," said Foster, who had never seen a dumbwaiter in his life.

"Maybe for children?" Davey wondered.

"Well, come on. What are we waiting for?" invited Foster; and he hiked himself up and into the box of the dumbwaiter. "Come on in, Dave; there's room for two if we sit kind of squeezy."

Davey fitted himself in by Foster. It was rich with dust in there, but by now they were very much at home with dust, so who cared. They had to sit cross-legged and pull in their elbows, and if they had been a few years older, they would have had to bend their heads down, too, but as it was they fitted very well.

Foster grasped the prickly hemp rope that hung

at one side, gave it a tug, and with a croak and a wobble, their elevator rose up in the shaft.

"Man!" cried Davey in delight. "Give her another yank, Foss, and see if she goes up to the roof!"

It was dark as they went up the shaft, but not badly dark, not pitch dark, because the door below stood open, letting in the light.

Foster maneuvered the dumbwaiter up as far as it would go: to another door on the next story, but there was no latch on the inside, so of course they couldn't open it. Then they went down to the first floor and then up again. The ascending box lurched pleasantly on its rope, knocking against the walls of the shaft now and then and creaking and croaking as it went.

"Up to Pluto, up to the moon!" cried Foster.

"Up to the moon in an old soup spoon!" sang Davey, in a burst of inspiration.

This seemed so terribly funny to them both that they began to giggle.

They reached the top of the shaft again with a bump, and paused there in the exciting darkness that was not dark enough to be scary.

"Up to the moon in an old jelly spoon!" sang Foster, and the giggles redoubled.

At that very instant, outdoors on the front porch, Mr. Caduggan and Joe Baskerville, after a mighty effort and some strong language, managed to force the great front door to open at last. It swung in heavily, rustily, with a slow reluctant groan, and as it gave way, the March wind entered, blew in a current through the hall and the dining room, finally reached the pantry, and firmly slammed the dumb-waiter door.

Total blackness in the shaft.

The giggles stopped abruptly.

"*Hey!*" yelled Davey.

"Ma-a-a!" yelled Foster. "*Daddy!*"

They called and called, but no one heard them. After a while, because it seemed the only thing to do, they began to cry.

Portia, coming upstairs to refresh herself with a look at her beloved round room, heard most curious noises: a keening and wailing and then some thumps. But where were they coming from? Where in the world? She listened a moment, then hurried into her parents' room: the big one that had belonged to Mrs. Brace-Gideon herself.

But the room was empty.

Empty of people, that is. Otherwise, it was occupied by large furniture, large mirrors, and on the wall opposite the door a large square oil painting of a motherly-looking barefoot lady wearing a Grecian robe and balancing a sort of pitcher on her shoulder. In the background, above an arrangement of sheep and ruins, fat pink sunset clouds swam in a school.

"Ma-a-a! Boo-hoo!" came the wail, directly it seemed, from the picture itself or from the wall behind it.

Portia felt her scalp creep and, turning, ran from the room, through the hall, and down the stairs, calling in her turn.

"Mother! Daddy! Mother! Daddy!"

Oh, I don't want it to be a ghost, she thought. Oh, I don't want our lovely house to be haunted!

Her mother, holding a ruler and a pair of pliers, emerged from the drawing room. Her father, holding a monkey wrench and a can of machine oil, came bounding up from the cellar stairs.

"What is it, Portia?"

"Upstairs, upstairs—oh, I hope it isn't a ghost—somebody's crying in the wall!"

"*What?*"

"Listen! Just listen!"

With their faces turned toward the ceiling they listened. Faintly, they heard the wailing.

"That's not a ghost; that's Foster!" declared Mrs. Blake, running for the stairs. Her husband and daughter were close behind.

"In your room," Portia directed, and when they

entered it, her father and mother were as puzzled as she had been.

"But there's nobody . . . *Foster!*" called Mrs. Blake. "Where are you, darling? Can you hear me?"

"We—we're in here. In the elevator thing," gulped Foster's voice, right behind the sheep-lady's picture.

"Oho!" said Mr. Blake, with the tone of one who is inspired. He leaped across the room to the picture and ran his fingers along the heavy gilt frame. "Fake!" he exclaimed. "I thought so! It's not a picture hanging on a wall; it's a door!"

His searching fingers found the partially concealed latch on the right side of the frame, and after the usual struggle of wrenching and tugging, managed to open the picture-door. Foster and Davey, two dirty owls, blinked in the sudden light, tear tracks shining on their cheeks.

"Oh, darling!" cried Mrs. Blake, hugging Foster out of the dumbwaiter; then she reached for Davey and hugged him out, too.

"Great Scott, those ropes are *ancient!*" said Mr. Blake. "Thank the Lord they didn't fail! Luckily they were closed away from the weather all this time. Otherwise—" But he left the sentence unfinished.

Mrs. Blake was so relieved that she began to scold. "Never again, Foster, do you hear? *Never!* It was a dreadfully stupid thing to do! Those ropes are more than fifty years old: maybe even sixty or sixty-five! They might very well have broken, and then—" But she, too, left the sentence unfinished and gave her son another hug instead.

Foster was so relieved that he began to boast. "It was neat! I yanked that old jalopy up till it hit the top, bang! And then I yanked it down till it hit the bottom, bang! And then I yanked it up again, and I bet that old jalopy never went so fast before. It was neat, wasn't it, Dave?"

"Ye-es," Davey said. "But I guess we better never do it again."

"Nope," said Foster soberly, remembering the pitch-black shaft. "I guess we better never."

"But why in the world do you suppose Mrs. Brace-Gideon had a dumbwaiter landing in her bedroom?" Portia asked. "And why did she hide it with that picture?"

"Mrs. Brace-Gideon was a lady of leisure," her mother said. "She probably took her breakfast in bed. The dumbwaiter would bring her tray up each morning, nice and hot, from the kitchen pantry."

"And the painting, no doubt, was put there to conceal a plain functional door with what she considered to be a thing of beauty," said Mr. Blake, studying the picture.

Portia thought of the dumbwaiter and the sheep-lady, and Baron Bloodshed, and the crystal chandelier, and all the other curious or lovely things they had discovered.

"What a place!" she said thoughtfully. "You know what this house is, Mother? Daddy? It is a house of astonishment!"

6

The House of Astonishment

It was indeed a house of astonishment. The day before the last day of spring vacation, Mr. Caduggan, who had been having what he called "a jawb" getting the attic door open, finally *did* get it open and mounted the steep stairs beyond it carefully, testing the treads.

A few minutes after he had reached the top he came licketty-splitting down again, with Popeye at his heels in a three-legged run.

"Mrs. Blake, Mrs. Blake!" shouted Mr. Caduggan. "Oh, Mrs. Bla-ake!"

Portia was startled from her room by his intemperate bellows, and Mr. Caduggan drew up short at sight of her.

"Where's your mama, Portia?"

"In the pantry looking over the china, I think," Portia said. "Why? What is it? What's the matter?"

But Mr. Caduggan was already on his way down

the next flight of stairs, with Popeye just behind him, barking impulsively. Portia followed, of course, and Julian joined them in the front hall.

"What goes? Is the house afire?"

"I don't know," Portia said. "I guess not or he'd say so."

They ran after him through the hall, through the dining room, to the pantry. Popeye barked.

Mrs. Blake and Aunt Hilda turned from their work, startled by the racket, and Aunt Hilda nearly dropped a teacup.

"What in the *world?*" said Mrs. Blake.

"Well, I tell you, ma'am," Mr. Caduggan said gustily, heaving with mystery and importance. "If you'll just step up-attic for a minute, I think there's something there you'll want to see."

Foster and Davey, who had been in the laundry, sitting cozily in a washtub reading comics, dislodged themselves and came to find out what was happening.

"What in the *world?*" repeated Mrs. Blake, dusting her hands on her dusty apron. "What can it be, Mr. Caduggan?"

"I'd rather you saw for yourself, ma'am," he replied cryptically.

"Is it something good or something bad?" Portia pleaded as they all mounted the stairs to the second floor.

"Wait and see," said Mr. Caduggan.

"Is it something dangerous?" asked Foster, alight with hope.

"Is it a live thing?" asked Davey. And then he asked in a lower tone: "Is it a *dead* thing?"

"Wait and see," replied Mr. Caduggan imperturbably.

At the attic door he turned and said: "One at a time, please, up these stairs. They ain't none too steady. Need bracin'. Mrs. Blake, you first, ma'am."

Mrs. Blake ran lightly up the wooden steps, then Aunt Hilda, then the children (Julian first, as usual).

It was dim "up-attic" and like the rest of the house, full of objects and full of dust. Mr. Caduggan went to a window and ripped off the dark and rotting window shade.

"There," said he.

Mrs. Blake drew in her breath. So did Aunt Hilda.

"Duncan Phyfe!" exclaimed Mrs. Blake, in the low voice of awe.

"Duncan who? I don't see *anybody*," Foster said.

"Chippendale!" exclaimed Aunt Hilda. "Can it really be? But it is, it is! Oh, Barbara, look! Queen Anne!"

Portia and Julian wondered if their mothers had gone mad.

"Are they talking about all those old bureaus

and things?" Foster demanded; he could see that they were, and he was disgusted. Downstairs the house was a regular furniture store, it was so full of tables and sofas and chairs and desks; and now here was all this excitement about still *more* furniture. He could not understand it.

Mr. Caduggan attempted to explain. "Well, see, the furniture up here is real old; what they call antique, see. It's like two hundred years old, give a little take a little, and what's more it was made when folks knew how to *make* furniture. My dad was a cabinetmaker, and his dad before him. I learned about good furniture from them. Look at this, for instance; this is real fine work: satinwood inlay. My, my, look at that work."

Portia could see that the pieces were beautifully made, beautifully ornamented with carved shapes of shells, urns, even of flames. But Julian inclined toward Foster's view.

"Still, it's only furniture," was his judgment. "If it was gold or jewels or Greek statues, or something, I could understand it. But just a lot of old furniture when you've *got* a lot of old furniture—I don't see why it's so great."

"Look, my young realist," Mrs. Blake said. "Regard it in this light. The tall cabinet over there with the urn-shaped finials is called a highboy. Aside from its beauty, it is extremely valuable. If I can

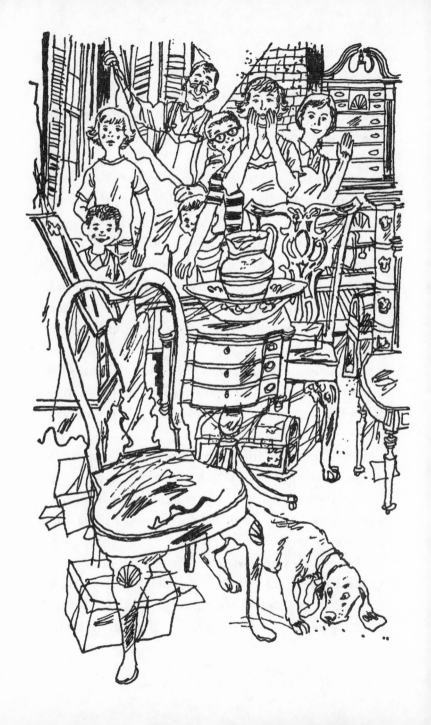

ever bear to part with it, it will not only pay the bill for all the new copper piping this house must have, it will probably pay for the entire electric system as well. And that is only *one* among these priceless things . . ."

"Wow!" Julian conceded.

"And of course I will have to part with some of them," his aunt continued. "As you know, the Blake family is far from rich. What Mr. Caduggan has discovered is not only a treasure-trove; it is a life-saver!"

The children looked at the furniture with new respect after that, though it was impossible for them to take great interest in it. Enthusiasm concerning furniture is something that belongs to grownups. Mrs. Blake and Aunt Hilda were in a trance of joy, prowling about among the pieces, opening little doors and drawers, exclaiming with wonder and delight. No less engrossed and pleased was Popeye, lured hither and thither by a stimulating age-old smell of mouse. He snuffled, scuffled, whined, and scratched, thoroughly contented.

Foster pushed his way between objects to the dormer window. From this he could look down with a new eye at "The Property"—leafless bushes, ragged loop of drive, brown slopes studded with crocuses. Eli Scaynes rounded the corner trundling a wheelbarrow full of sticks and twigs. He looked very small, and so did Julian's dog, Othello, sniffing about in the orchard. Neither knew that anyone was watching him, and that made each of them look lonesome.

"Come on, Dave; let's go outdoors," said Foster, and the two of them went pounding down the stairs.

"But why do you suppose Mrs. Brace-Gideon kept all those marvels in the attic?" Mrs. Blake wondered.

"Well, judging from the way she furnished her house, these simply weren't to her taste," Aunt Hilda said. "Not fashionable enough, probably."

Besides the furniture, this part of the attic was crowded with a great collection of bedroom crockery, pitchers, basins, bowls of all sizes and shapes; boxes piled on boxes, and trunks on trunks; there was another dressmaker's dummy, rather stouter than Baron Bloodshed; there was an agitated-looking sewing machine, an agitated-looking typewriter, both rusty; and a large, elaborate bird cage that must once have housed a parrot.

"Things and things to look at and discover, all summer long." Portia gloated. "Now where does this door go, I wonder?"

"Well, let's find out."

The door was at the end of the attic storeroom. Julian turned the handle and gave a shove; for a wonder it yielded easily.

Opening off a narrow corridor were six small rooms, three to a side, each with an iron bedstead, a washstand, a small looking glass, and a mouse-trap. The little rooms smelled musty and dry, the wallpaper was stained, and fallen plaster lay on the floors. Portia found a broken rosary in one room, and on the wall of another there was a tacked-up faded postal card, showing the picture of a lighthouse. It looked very forlorn.

"I guess this is where she kept her servants," Julian said.

"In these horrid little rooms?" Portia was shocked. "Why, they're like the rooms in a jail!"

But then she remembered the tale of how Mrs. Brace-Gideon had been in the habit of acquiring two kittens for pets each summer, and then when it was time to return to the city, she would take them to the vet's and have them chloroformed (until Baby-Belle Tuckertown had outwitted her).

"I think Mrs. Brace-Gideon was a—was a—what's that word that means you do whatever you want no matter who doesn't want you to?" Portia demanded.

"Ruthless?"

"Yes. I think she must have been a *ruthless, ruthless* lady!"

"Aunt Minnehaha says she wasn't so bad," Julian said. "Just too rich to understand much. Anyway, lots of people treated their servants that way in those days."

Portia looked at the narrow corridor, at the narrow, neglected rooms. They made her feel dreary, as though other people's dreariness still lingered there.

"Well, I know *one* thing," she said. "Someday, I'm going to fix these rooms up so they'll look cheerful."

That afternoon Portia and Julian were dispatched to Gone-Away to invite Mrs. Cheever for a cup of tea.

"If anyone knows why those beautiful things are stuck away in the attic, she will," said Mrs. Blake.

And it was true. After they had escorted Mrs. Cheever back and after she had cautiously mounted the attic stairs and done her share of grown-up furniture-worshiping, they all returned to the drawing room for tea poured out of a Thermos bottle, and she told them what she remembered.

"It all comes back to me, now," Mrs. Cheever said, holding her teacup daintily and watching its fragrant steam. "Yes, yes, indeed it does. Mrs. Brace-Gideon had two houses, you know: this one for summertime, and another still grander—oh, very grand, a mansion!—in Pittsburgh. Shortly before she died, she sold the Pittsburgh house with the intention of removing to California for the winters. (That is how she happened to be in San Francisco at the time of the earthquake.) And it seems to me—yes, I do recollect—that she sold the house furnished, except for some very old pieces in the attic. They were not to her taste at all, oh, not at all, but they had been in the family for generations, so out of sentiment she kept them . . ."

"Thank fortune," said Mrs. Blake.

"Thank fortune," agreed Mrs. Cheever. "Family sentiment, yes, of course, but no doubt her shrewd eye for value played a part, too. . . . So she stored them here (temporarily, she thought). . . . Now as I recall, the American pieces, the Duncan Phyfe and so on, had belonged to her grandmother—I *think* it was her grandmother—but I *know* that all the rest had been brought in a sailing vessel clear around the Horn by her great-grandfather, a Captain Deuteronomy Dadware. I remember his name because how could one possibly forget it?"

Mrs. Cheever sipped her tea delicately. She was wearing a crimson wool dress, a high lace collar, and many long chains of beads. The bow that always sailed on top of her crimped white hair was the same color as her dress. The walk in the March wind and now the hot tea had caused a wintry pinkness to come into her cheeks. She looked very nice, Portia and Julian thought. They were sitting cross-legged on the floor, drinking their own tea and eating whatever was available.

"Aunt Minnehaha, was Mrs. Brace-Gideon what you would call a ruthless woman?" Portia asked.

"In certain ways she was, yes, indeed she was," replied Mrs. Cheever decisively. "She was very determined. She not only wanted to have her own way; she simply *had* to *have* her own way, and because of her strong will and her great wealth she very often got it. Nature, weather particularly, was a severe trial to her because it simply would not comply or submit. When we had bad spells of rain or cold, my father said it must be harder on Mrs. Brace-Gideon than anybody because she couldn't do a thing about it. She couldn't write to the management or to the *New York Times*. She couldn't fire anybody or bribe anybody. She, with all her money, had to live through bad weather just like the beggar in his hut.

"*But*," continued Mrs. Cheever, "she was just when she saw that justice was required, and she was very brave.

"One day, one of her maids, Nelly, fell off the end of a Gone-Away dock—I forget how—into deep water. She couldn't swim a stroke and was beginning to gulp and go under, but Mrs. Brace-Gideon stood on the end of the dock and shouted: 'Nelly, I forbid you to drown! I forbid it! You wait right there!'

"And do you know Nelly didn't drown because she didn't dare to; she managed to keep her head above water somehow until Mrs. Brace-Gideon— *who couldn't swim a stroke either, mind you!*—jumped right into the lake wearing her hat and holding her parasol, in all her heavy clothes and her heavy corsets and her heavy jewelry! It's a wonder she ever came up again, but she did, thank fortune, and clinging to a piling, she reached out her parasol so that Nelly, poor creature, could grasp it and be towed in. Then Mrs. Brace-Gideon, holding on to Nelly with one arm and the piling with the other, began calling for help in the loud, strong operatic voice she had, and everybody heard her and came running. My father said he never forgot Mrs. Brace-Gideon being hoisted out of the lake still wearing her big wide picture hat. In those days, of course, ladies' hats were always skewered on with hatpins."

"I wish I'd seen her," Julian said.

"What other brave things did she do?" Portia wanted to know.

"Well, one night—haven't I told you this? But no, I'm sure I haven't—one night, when she couldn't sleep, she became aware of a sound downstairs, a very small but suspicious sound. It was late—oh, I think two or three o'clock!—so she got up, put on one of the magnificent dressing gowns she had, and tiptoed out to listen. . . . Well, sure enough, she heard the sound again, whatever it was like, a sort of careful clinking or chinking, I imagine, and she was convinced it was a robber!

"So she crept down the stairs. *Crept!* For such a commanding woman, she could be very quiet when she needed to. . . . A light was coming faintly from the drawing room—this very room (or so she said). . . . At the foot of the stairs she picked up that cast-iron pug-dog doorstop—you know the one?"

"*I* do," Julian said feelingly. "I tripped over it and fell down, hard, the first time I ever came exploring in this house!"

"Then you know how solid it is. So Mrs. Brace-Gideon tiptoed to the drawing-room door and peeked in, and *there*, *yes*, there *was* a man—a *burglar*—kneeling on the floor, with a dark lantern beside him and a pistol in one hand! And the door of the safe was open before him!"

"A safe? You mean it? In this very room?" Julian's eyes were shooting sparks.

"Well, that's what she told *us*, Julian. But you must remember that Mrs. Brace-Gideon was not what one would call a trusting person; no, she was not. So the safe may very well have been concealed in some other room. However, the rest of the story is absolutely true. Every bit of it."

"So she saw this burglar . . ." Portia prompted breathlessly.

"So she saw him. She was a large woman, as you know: imposing. And I am sure that outrage must have made her twice as large, twice as imposing! . . . Well, she stepped quietly up to this creature, this burglar, and she said: '*Halt!* I command you to *halt!*' Oh, she had an imperious voice! It could be terrible when she was giving orders . . .

"The poor burglar was so startled that he dropped the pistol, and Mrs. Brace-Gideon, with great presence of mind, moved in and put her foot on it firmly, and then she hit him on the head with the cast-iron pug dog! Well, over he went, just plain keeled over on the floor, entirely unconscious. And while he *was* unconscious, she went to the windows, ripped off the portiere cords, and bound him up with them, trussed him up tight like a good rolled roast, and when that was done—and the safe closed up again, I'll be bound—she began ringing bells for the servants as hard as she could. The coachman was sent for the constable; the burglar, still unconscious, was carried off to jail; and then, only *then*, Mrs. Brace-Gideon crossed her ankles gracefully and permitted herself to faint on the divan of the Turkish cozy corner!"

"Goodness!" said Mrs. Blake.

"I'm glad this house isn't haunted," Aunt Hilda declared. "I think Mrs. Brace-Gideon might have made a very dominating ghost."

Julian stood up, putting his cup and saucer on the tray.

"I'm just wondering about that safe, though," he said. "I mean maybe it's still here, somewhere. Would you mind if I sort of investigated, Aunt Barbara?"

"Do! By all means," said Mrs. Blake.

So from that moment, until it was time to escort Mrs. Cheever back to Gone-Away, Portia and Julian prowled and crouched about the room, tapping at the walls and wainscoting, testing the floorboards, feeling around picture frames for concealed catches—"because it just might be behind a picture door, like the sheep-lady door," Julian said.

But their search was to no avail.

"Never mind," said Mrs. Cheever, as they walked back through the windy dusk. "Just as I told you, Mrs. Brace-Gideon was not a trustful person. No, she was not. I am certain she would never have told anybody where the safe truly was; or if she had to tell them truly at the time, she would then have moved it elsewhere. You may still find it, children, but I doubt there'll be a penny in it."

"It's just that it's fun to look," Julian explained. "It's fun to think about."

"Oh, I *wish* I didn't have to go back to the horrible, loathsome, disgusting old city!" Portia groaned.

"Never mind," Mrs. Cheever said again. "Think of how beautiful it will be when you come back: all the reeds of Gone-Away tipping and swishing, and the redwings calling, and the bullfrogs grumping, and the roses just— Oh, I declare I can hardly wait for it myself! No matter how old a person gets, he's never old in spring!"

Only three of them, Foster and Portia and Mr. Blake, took the train from Creston the next morning. Mrs. Blake would have to stay behind for several weeks until the house was in more livable shape.

Portia and Foster would miss their mother, of course, but they knew they wouldn't fare too badly. Mrs. Bryant would clean the house each morning. Mr. Blake knew how to cook steaks, chops, hamburgers, and hot dogs. He could also bake a potato. Portia knew how to cook pancakes and fudge. Foster knew how to make chocolate milk. As for Gulliver, his food came out of a can.

"So we'll be all right, we'll be fine," Mr. Blake assured his wife.

"Of course you will, I know you will," she said. "But, Paul darling, do see that Foster really *brushes* his teeth, not just strokes them. And do watch him with the catsup. If you let him, he'd pour it on his food the way Vesuvius poured lava on Pompeii. I don't see how he knows what he's eating. And then about Portia—"

But fortunately for Portia, the train arrived at that moment.

From its windows, after only ten days, the country they traveled through already seemed less the property of winter. All the snow patches were gone, and the trees, especially the willows, showed a color of life in their twigs.

"It won't really be very long before we come back," Portia said, to comfort both herself and Foster. "It only seems long."

"That's just the same as being," Foster said.

7

Another Beginning

But at last it was June. At last school was over and summer, huge as an ocean, lay before them.

"September is forever away!" sang Portia, sitting on her suitcase to shut it. "Forever and ever and ever away!"

This time when they returned to the country, Gulliver went with them because they drove there. They drove in their own brand-new car: "Bought," as Mrs. Blake explained to Julian later, "by courtesy of the Sheraton octagonal drum table." She sighed when she said it: she had hated parting with the drum table. "But if we're going to have a house in the country miles from any town, we must have a car."

"And that's the only way we could afford it," Portia added, "because of buying the house and fixing it up and all."

They made the journey on a wonderful day: June

at its most fragrant and expansive. Foster, to the relief of all, seemed to have outgrown his car sickness; and Gulliver, about whom there had been some doubt, proved to be a courteous passenger, neither trampling nor barking.

It was late afternoon when they turned in at the gates of the Villa Caprice. The road and driveway had been partly reclaimed from the woods, but were still far from smooth; the going was very jouncy. Emerging, finally, from the shade of new-leafed trees, the Blakes were surprised and charmed by what they saw. Eli Scaynes had made great headway with "The Property." The grass had been cut, and large areas of lawn were newly seeded. Bushes had been pruned, brush and brambles cleared away.

"It still looks wild, but sort of *neatly* wild," Portia said approvingly.

And the house looked so different! The porch was gone; the vine had been trimmed and the shutters painted. It was not beautiful, but it looked respectable. And in spite of looking respectable, it looked interesting.

"It's not a training school for witches anymore, is it?" said Mr. Blake.

"No," Foster agreed. "Now it's a people's house."

Mr. Blake took one hand from the wheel and put his arm around Mrs. Blake's shoulders.

"Barbara, you've worked a miracle," he told her.

"Wait till you see the inside," said Mrs. Blake rather boastfully.

As they drove up to the house, the front door opened and down the broad shallow steps that had replaced the porch came all the Jarmans: Uncle Jake, Aunt Hilda, Julian, and their dogs, Katy and Othello, who had come to welcome Gulliver.

There was a turmoil of barkings, greetings, and embracings. Foster, grinning self-consciously at Julian, displayed the ingenuous gap where his two front teeth had been. (For at last, at last they had come out! A friend at school had recommended the biting of an apple, and this, though painful for a moment, had done the trick.)

"Holy crow," said Julian, "you look just like an adder!" Then he pretended to cower away. "Take cover, men; it is the Fang!" he warned. Foster was pleased.

"But come in, come in! Welcome to your own house," Aunt Hilda said, holding the big door open.

The first thing they saw was a great burst of peonies on the hall table. Aunt Hilda had filled the house with flowers, and it did look lovely, especially the drawing room, which was freshly painted, light, clean, and airy despite the large and curious assortment of furniture. The walls were white; the polished floor was the color of honey; overhead the chandelier twinkled and tinkled, and through the windows came a smell of lilies of the valley.

"I don't see why all these things go together so well," Uncle Jake objected. "There's absolutely no reason why they should."

But they did. The graceful Chippendale highboy looked perfectly at home with the boisterous red and gold piano. The curving Sheraton cabinet seemed

entirely suited to the gilded chairs, the bamboo curtain, and the harp. The harp was so pretty that they had had to keep it, though nobody, as yet, knew how to play it.

Above the mantel hung a portrait of Mrs. Brace-Gideon; a well-corseted lady with a pink, opinionated face. She was sitting bolt upright in a chair, wearing an embroidered gown and holding a fan.

"And there she is going to stay," said Mrs. Blake.

"Because in her way, and though she could never know it, Mrs. Brace-Gideon has been a fairy godmother to this family."

"Indeed she has," said Mr. Blake.

When Portia went upstairs to look at her own round room in the turret, she screamed with delight.

"Mother, how did you *know* I wanted pink?"

"All girls want pink," replied her mother sensibly.

Just under the curving open window a giant rhododendron had put out hundreds of bouquets of flowers, delicately tinted: not quite white, less definite than pink.

"How lucky that they should turn out to be that color instead of the usual magenta," Mrs. Blake mused, sitting on the window seat and leaning her arms on the sill. "How lucky, really, about everything."

"I know," Portia said, staring dreamily out over her mother's head at the green lawn, the green orchard, the green woods beyond.

Their mood of quiet delight was shattered by a tremendous outburst of rushing waters. It was Foster trying out the plumbing to see if it would work.

"Hey, everybody, the plumbing's working!" he shouted, somewhat unnecessarily. "Come on and see this cool bathroom!"

For some reason Portia had overlooked the

bathroom up to now, and it did turn out to be an interesting place: very large, with two high-up diamond-shaped windows, a frieze of mildewed swans above the molding, and many pictures on the wall of young ladies wearing pompadours, shirtwaists, and long skirts, like Mrs. Cheever's.

The hand basin, made of Delft china, was patterned with blue carnations. Swan-necked faucets drooped above it, and on each side there was a broad slab of marble, veined and gray as Roquefort cheese. Traces of ancient soap lay in an ancient dish; and, hung above the basin, an oval mirror offered a green and speckled face to anyone who looked in it.

The bathtub was immense, porcelain encased in solid mahogany. "Sort of like a coffin," Foster said. He would enjoy a bath in this from time to time, he thought. It was so huge, he might be able to swim a stroke or two.

The chain by which he had recently released the uproar was attached to a large tank high above the thronelike fixture, which stood nobly upon its own gray marble slab.

"Yipes, it's the loudest one I ever heard," Foster said in awe, giving the chain another pull and releasing another crashing avalanche of sound.

"This is much better than a new-time bathroom," he shouted above the tumult.

Curious, Portia opened the door of a cabinet

hanging on the wall and began to examine the bottles with dried-up medicines and lotions in them: the round bronze-colored paper pillboxes containing petrified pills. From time to time she read a label out loud.

" 'Mrs. Baggett's Bunion Balm,' " she read, and then: " 'Dr. Cupthorn's Efficacious Cough Deterrent, for the cure of coughs, colds, bronchitis, asthma, influenza, wasting diseases, and scrofulous humours!' I wonder what those are?"

"Scrofulous humours," Foster murmured dreamily, as he tried out the bathtub faucets (very slow and trickly). "Scrofulous humours, scrofulous humours."

"And listen to this: 'Princess Razzioli's Celebrated Elixir of Cucumber and Milkweed, for the Preservation of Pulchritude and a Pearly Complexion'!"

"Porsh, where are you?" came Julian's voice from the hall.

"In here reading medicines," Portia called in reply. "Come on in. Mr. Ormond Horton hasn't got around to painting the bathroom yet, so everything's just the way it was."

"Listen to this," Foster said, and gave the chain another pull. Julian was suitably impressed; he said it sounded like a thunderstorm on the Maine coast.

When the racket had subsided, giving way to a series of low mutterings and garglings, Julian's face assumed a serious, intent expression. He began to prowl about the room, stopping to lean against the wall and listen as he rapped it with his knuckles.

"What in the world are you doing?" Portia demanded.

"Well, a safe could be hidden anywhere, couldn't it? Even in a bathroom, couldn't it?"

Julian stooped to open the door of the cupboard beneath the hand basin. Nothing in there but rusty cans of cleaning powder and some stubbed-off scrub brushes.

"Oh, that old safe! You've got that old safe on the brain, Jule. I'd forgotten all about it. And I bet you we'll never find it; she probably buried it under an apple tree, or sent it out to California, or threw it in the well, or something. Anyway, come on; let's go outside," Portia said. "I'm tired of this old bathroom. I'm tired of indoors; I want outdoors."

"All right," Julian agreed willingly enough. "We'll keep the safe-hunting for rainy days. I'm not going to give up, though. Come on, Fang, come outdoors with us."

"O.K.," said Foster gladly, and all three went pelting down the stairs, where children had never pelted until now.

It was very early when Portia woke up the next morning; the birds woke her. Every bird on earth was singing, it seemed. She had never heard such a jingling and jangling in her life.

Getting up, she went to the window to look out at the flowering, loudly singing world, and decided to go for a walk in her pajamas.

Everyone else was still asleep, so she tiptoed down the stairs, past the suit of armor on the landing that looked just as if it had a real knight inside it, and past the bronze lady who stood poised on the newel post. The bronze lady was called Miss McCurdy because she bore a striking resemblance to a live lady of this name who was a cashier at the Blue Premium Grocery Store in Pork Ferry.

Gulliver came yawning and stretching from the kitchen.

"We're going for a walk," Portia told him.

When she had unbolted and opened the big front door, Gulliver bounded out and went racing around the lawn in a dance of circles, but Portia walked slowly down the broad new steps, sniffing the air. M-m-m, lilies of the valley. She let her nose lead her to where they grew, spread in a vast green carpet under the apple trees. I was sure they'd all be gone by now, she thought. Of course then she had to stop and pick a big wet bunch of them, admiring their crispness and freshness: each little staff of bells trimmed with two broad leaves, like rabbits' ears.

The air rang with the energetic, joyful clamor of the birds. Only one, whose song came sweetly through the others, sounded meditative and solitary: three minor notes ascending. She wondered what it was.

A lively clanking caused her to turn her head: there came Julian along the drive, his camera, his field glasses, his collecting case, his lunch box, and a small canteen all draped about his person. No wonder he clanked more than usual.

"So early?" Portia said, surprised.

"The birds. I'm used to them, but they even woke me up, so I was positive they'd wake *you* up. I thought we'd better get started early; we've got a lot of work to do."

"We have?"

"Why, sure. We have to get the club fixed up, don't we? No one's cleaned it since September."

"Good," Portia said; that was the one sort of housecleaning she enjoyed. "And Mother's given us some things from here to decorate it with!"

"Great. Foster can help carry."

Through the tangles of singing came the one sweet song.

"What's that bird, Jule? That sort of sad one?"

Julian listened. "White-throated sparrow," he told her. Honestly, that boy knows everything, Portia thought, but she didn't say so.

"I wish it had a prettier name." She sighed. "Hear how pretty it sounds."

"One's all right, maybe . . . yes, it sounds nice, it really does . . . but a bunch of them together can drive you nuts."

There was never more than one, though, all that month, and every day Portia listened for its song. It meant something special to her, perhaps because it was the little music of this first lovely morning . . .

Finally the racket of the birds even got through to Foster, and he woke up. Hearing conversation just below his window, he hopped up and looked out to see his sister and his cousin; then he, also in his pajamas, ran down the stairs and out-of-doors to join them.

"Hi, Fang!" Julian greeted him. "How are you today?"

"I have scrofulous humours," Foster said.

"You have *what?*"

"Something she read off a bottle," Foster explained, indicating his sister. "I haven't really got them. I don't think I have."

"I don't think so either."

"Well, I'm going up to dress," Portia said. "My pajama legs are soaked with dew. Have you had breakfast, Jule?"

"Ye-es." Julian sounded doubtful. "But—"

"But you could eat another one, you mean?"

"If Aunt Barbara wouldn't mind . . ."

"Oh, she won't mind, she never does. I think I could eat two myself. And afterwards—you help me with the dishes, Jule—and after that we'll go to Gone-Away and see about the club. It's probably a perfect mess," Portia said contentedly, and went singing into the house.

8

Gone-Away Housekeeping

All the length of the drive, until it curved into the woods, Portia kept turning around and walking backward so she could watch her house.

"Remember last year just about now when Aunt Minnehaha told us about the Villa Caprice and said it gave her the creeps? And remember how it gave us the creeps first time we saw it? Well, just look at it now, Jule. Did you ever see anything so changed in all your life?"

Julian walked backward, too, for a minute; so did Foster and so did Davey, who had arrived as soon after breakfast as his mother would let him.

"And it's not even finished yet," Portia said.

They could see Mr. Caduggan up on a ladder putting a screen on a window. Joe Baskerville was putting on another. Popeye was sitting down watching them, and Gulliver was sitting down watching Popeye.

Mr. Ormond Horton had just arrived in his old pickup truck and was assembling his paint buckets, singing melodiously as he did so.

At the far end of the house, Eli Scaynes was down on his knees, setting out pansies. His faithful wheelbarrow waited at his side, with a rake and a shovel sticking out of it.

"I like to see neglected houses getting fixed," Portia said. "Of course I know houses can't possibly think, but sometimes I have a feeling they can *feel*. Do you ever, Jule?"

"Nope," said Julian, "I sure as heck don't."

He was no longer alone in his clanking. They all clanked. Everyone had a lunch box, and Portia in addition had a large basket filled with donations from the Villa Caprice. Julian had another. As for the two little boys, they were burdened with buckets and brushes. They were not carrying these things because they wished to but because that was the condition under which they had been allowed to come.

Foster permitted himself a grumble or two, but the day was so dazzling, the air was so ravishing, that the grumbles dried up in spite of him.

Emerging from the woods where everything seemed to be flying and singing, the four children approached the old houses of Gone-Away from the rear. In the weedy wastes that had once been gardens or backyards were relics left from an earlier

day: the vine-trapped sleigh behind the Humboldt house, clothes posts silvered by a thousand weathers, the slatted skeleton of an old lawn swing. Some of the fences remained, half lost in weeds, with many of their pickets missing, like giant combs with broken teeth.

"Look, the barn swallows are nesting in Judge Chater's house again this year!"

"Swallows hate to change their habits," Julian said. "They're worse than grownups."

The fork-tailed birds, azure-blue in the sunlight, swooped and curved in and out of the tottering cupola that crowned the decaying mansion. They used the air as fishes use a river; they seemed to swing and spin effortlessly on invisible currents.

"If I had to be a bird, I'd be a swallow," Foster

said. "They have the best time flying. They look as if they do."

"If you were a bird, you'd have to eat bugs," Davey told him. "You'd have to eat worms. You'd *like* to eat worms. Oig. If anybody told me I had to be a bird, I wouldn't."

At the Tuckertown house they set their burdens down on the front doorstep. They had decided before getting down to work to pay a call first to Mr. Payton, because his house was nearest, and then to Mrs. Cheever.

"Because it's the polite thing to do," Julian said, his courteous Gone-Away manners descending on him like a mantle.

"And anyway because we want to," Foster added. "Check."

Feeling as light as the swallows, now that their hands were free, the children ran along the footpath that lay between the Gone-Away houses and the swamp, connecting Mr. Payton's house at the extreme right to Mrs. Cheever's house at the extreme left.

As they neared Mr. Payton's house, a faint smell of goat was wafted toward them, mingling with all the other smells: roses, fresh grass, swamp water.

"Wind's from the north," Julian commented, not without logic, since Mr. Payton's house was at the north end of Gone-Away and he kept goats.

They found him busy in his vegetable garden at the far side of his house. The rows of vegetables, perfectly straight, were stripes of various greens except for two, which were strangely covered up with cloth.

"Good morning, good morning!" Mr. Payton called, delighted to see them. He took off his broad-brimmed hat, waving it in a flourish of welcome.

"Ma-a-a," called Uncle Sam, the billy goat, from his pen near the woods. Perhaps he meant it as a greeting.

"May I offer anyone a radish? Or a spring onion? Or a very young carrot? These are all my garden affords at present," Mr. Payton said, but for once nobody was hungry, not even Julian.

"We had waffles," Foster explained.

"Ah. Entirely understandable."

Near Mr. Payton's garden there was another just like it but without a fence around it. This was his rabbit or guest garden for animals. There was food there for any hungry rabbit, woodchuck, field mouse, or deer.

"To say nothing of the scoundrel blackbirds," he said with a frown. "*Those* rascals wait until the exact moment when the peas have reached perfection; then they walk along the rows and slit the pods with their bills, neat as if they were opening their mail, and there go your peas! Frustrating. Well, I tried everything. Scarecrows never scared them; I put a dozen pinwheels to a row; but they'd wait till the wind died down. Smart villains. Finally I struck on the idea of covering the peas in *my* garden with mosquito netting, as you see. Worked like a charm. Those birds can eat their own peas. Perfectly fair. But not mine. And it's a pleasure to frustrate *them* for a change!"

Fatly, the cat, came trotting along a furrow with his collar bell tinkling. He had the sleekness and softness of a healthy country cat. His eyes looked dazzled in the sunshine.

"I frustrate *him*, too, this time of year," Mr. Payton told them. "I feed him so handsomely each morning that he has no interest whatever in catching birds."

By this time, on a common impulse, they had moved away from the garden and were starting along the path in the direction of Mrs. Cheever's house. To the right of them, the wall of new reeds rippled and shivered; to the left, in the old dooryards, persistent garden flowers bloomed again: iris, peonies, poppies, roses.

As they walked, the children remarked on changes in the scene.

"The Delaneys' porch has finally fallen off."

"Look at that big fat wisteria vine on the Vogelharts' barn. I don't remember that."

"The turret on the Thompsons' house is much more sideways than it was."

Aunt Minnehaha's chickens came trotting, helter-skelter, to meet them; her duck, stepping on its own feet, waddled out from under its shade of dock leaves. "Everything is just like last year," Julian said. "Except it's better."

"I know," Portia agreed. "That's because it's ours now, in a way; or else because we're its."

No barking sounded from Mrs. Cheever's house. They found her kitchen empty, but the rustling range and the ticking clock made it seem occupied.

"She's in her bog garden, I'll be bound," Mr. Payton surmised, glancing into the square of looking glass above the sink and smoothing out his mustache. "Well, come along, Philosophers; we'll go and see."

"Her and Julian are Philosophers—" Foster started to say, but Portia interrupted him. "*She* and Julian, you mean, Foster."

"*She* and Julian are Philosophers, Uncle Pin, but me and Davey—"

"Foster! Davey and *I*," corrected his sister.

"—but Davey and *I* belong to another club, the Club of the Fang," Foster said proudly. "I'm the one that thought it up."

"I see. Very well then, come along, Philosophers and Fangs."

So they went out again, by the front door this time, and there, yes, there beyond the reeds, beyond the water meadow and the dead tree that marked the entrance to the bog, they spotted Mrs. Cheever's bell-shaped hat.

"Further I shall not go," Mr. Payton stated. "I do not care for wading and I've brought no boots. Minnie's busy in her garden, and I'll return to mine. Farewell, Philosophers. Farewell, Fangs."

"Good-bye, Uncle Pin."

Already the children were sitting on the ground, taking off their shoes and socks. Soon they were squelching cautiously through the forest of reeds. It was eventful walking. Frogs kept popping out of the way, and once something slithered and wriggled under Portia's foot.

"Man, can you squeal!" Julian said admiringly. "You sounded like the noon whistle at Pork Ferry."

"Well, heavens, I'm not in the habit of walking on snakes!"

Now they emerged from the reeds to the water meadow; Tarrigo saw them and came barking and splashing, sending showers of water sparks into the air.

Beyond, where water meadow turned to tufted bog, Mrs. Cheever stood waving to them with her trowel.

"Good morning, children, welcome! You're just

in time to see the arethusas; they've survived another winter, thank fortune."

Great banks of sheep laurel were in bloom, deep rose color—"beautiful, but poisonous," Mrs. Cheever said. "That's why it has that name. Sheep have grazed on it and died." Clumps of wild flag made blue islands in a sea already blue with blue-eyed grass; but the arethusas were pink, each growing by itself, its flower shaped like a tiny half-open hand. Portia admired every one of them, and after that every grass pink, and every pitcher plant. She prowled and stooped and examined, wading in and out of water. At this time of year, when brooks and ponds were cold as ice, the bog water, thin and open to the sun, was as warm as her own skin.

"I love this place," Portia said. "I love the smell of it. It smells like a jungle near the Orinoco, or someplace."

"Or like a hothouse," Julian said.

Actually it smelled like both those things: steamy, rich, tropical, healthy. And it had so much to offer! Rare flowers for those who were interested in them; bog butterflies for people who were lepidopterists, like Julian; snakes for people who were herpetologists, like his friend Tom Parks; frogs and turtles for people who were seven years old, like Foster and Davey.

"But I suppose we ought to go and start our housecleaning," Portia said regretfully.

"I guess so, and anyway the mosquitoes are beginning." Julian gave himself a vigorous slap.

"We forgot to put on your Anti-Pest Decoction," Portia told Mrs. Cheever, and slapped *herself*.

"Well, run along then, run along; you'll be devoured!"

"We have to clean our club, too," Foster said importantly. "Come on, Dave; we haven't got all day."

"Dirt is patient; it will wait," said Mrs. Cheever calmly. "That's *one* thing."

After they had filled a bucket with water at Mrs. Cheever's pump, Portia and Julian returned to Bellemere. They clattered up the stairs from the plaster-littered wreck of the first floor, to the shabby melancholy of the second, and then to the cozy attic, which was their clubhouse.

It was decidedly in need of attention. Dust was everywhere, and dead spiders dotted the floor. Their old webs hung from the rafters in deserted swags; seeing them, Portia hastily tied a dustcloth around her head; then she went to work on them with her broom. Julian attacked the floor with his.

"Next thing is scrubbing," he said.

"And after that the waxing."

"Yes. And then the windows."

"Oh, there's such an enormous amount to be *done*," Portia moaned, exactly as her mother had done about the Villa Caprice and sounding just as happy.

So the morning passed. They really did work hard, but every now and then, because it was simply impossible not to, they ran down the stairs and out into the blazing June sunshine; just to breathe and listen and feel.

At noon they borrowed the great conch shell that hung by Mrs. Cheever's door, and Julian blew a blast on it to summon Foster and Davey from their clubhouse on Craneycrow Island. In a moment the little boys could be heard drumming across the bridge above the Gulper. They had spent a satisfactory morning, after rapidly abandoning the idea of house-cleaning in favor of more congenial pursuits. They had lain on their stomachs on the bridge, dropping pebbles and watching the deadly Gulper suck them in; they had found ten new turtles for their turtlearium, all of which would soon escape; and they had conducted a frog hunt. In Foster's lunch box—he had prudently eaten his lunch early to make room for it—there was a bullfrog the size of a small puppy. Portia gave one of her noon-whistle squeals when she saw it.

"Listen; he's a very nice, gentle frog," Foster said reproachfully. "I'm going to keep him and raise him."

"He's already raised," Julian told Foster. "And if you keep him in captivity, he'll probably die."

"He will?" To their surprise, Foster looked rather relieved. "Well, O.K., I'll take him back and let him go then. Anyway, I was sort of afraid he'd scare me if he croaked in the night."

"He would have, too. That kind doesn't just croak; it goes off like a gun, boom!"

"You'll be all right; I'll let you go pretty soon," Foster told the frog; then he turned to his cousin. "I've named him already, though, and I named him after you: Julian Jarman Frog."

"Thanks a lot," Julian said. "I appreciate that a lot."

They ate their lunch lazily in the shade of the Vogelhart willow tree. Foster was persuaded to partake of a cooky. There was a noonday stillness on Gone-Away; only the red-winged blackbirds trilled and clucked, and the frog in the lunch box gave a sudden resounding boom.

"Yeeps!" said Foster. "He would have scared me all right."

After the little boys had departed, Julian and Portia lingered on, lying on their backs in the warm grass and looking straight into the sky.

"Not a cloud, not a bird, not a plane. Not a mosquito, even," Portia mused. "Just blue nothing. It makes you feel—I don't know—peaceful, I guess."

"M-m-m," Julian murmured noncommittally. It made him feel sleepy. He lay with his eyes half closed, chewing on a grass stem.

"Millions and trillions of miles of just blue nothing," Portia repeated dreamily. She liked that phrase.

"There goes a June bug, though. And up, way up, now, there's a hawk. And even if you can't see them, think of all the other things there are up there: satellites in orbit, meteors and meteorites, suns, moons, planets, stars; millions and billions and trillions of those! It doesn't make me feel peaceful, brother, it makes me feel nervous! 'Blue nothing,' *nothing!*"

"Honestly," was all Portia could think of to say to that.

Now a tiny plane went purring across the sky, very high, very slow to eyes grown accustomed to the flight of jets.

Portia lay thinking about the club. When they were through with the cleaning, and they almost were, they would decorate it with the things from the Villa Caprice: the painting of a starchily dressed young lady swinging on a crescent moon; the Tiffany glass lampshade (they had no lamp in the club, but if they turned the shade upside down, it would look like a vase, and it was a beautiful thing: all the colors of the rainbow, melted). They also had been given the cast-iron pug dog with which Mrs. Brace-Gideon had felled the burglar, and the procession of teakwood elephants, and many other treasures. When everything was in place, Portia would go out and pick a big bouquet of roses and iris, and that would be the finishing touch.

The distant plane made a peaceful, soothing sound. Very, very soothing . . .

Portia sat up abruptly and looked at her cousin.

"Jule, don't you *dare* go to sleep!" She began to tickle him mercilessly. "Wake up, wake up; we haven't finished working yet! Wake up this minute, Julian Jarman Frog!"

9

The Attic

Fine weather can't last forever. One morning, about a week later, Julian woke to a steady sound of rain.

"A good day to look for safes," he thought. He had spent the night at the Villa Caprice, as he would often do that summer. There were so many rooms in the house that there was also one for him.

"You must consider it your very own," his aunt had said, and this he was glad to do without a moment's hesitation.

It was a solemn, manly room with an enormous black bureau, an enormous black bed, an enormous black chair scratchily covered with horsehair. On the wall there was a steel engraving of the Roman Forum. Julian sat up and looked at his stately room. Othello, who had also spent the night, was lying on the oval rug before the fireplace. He suited the room admirably; he was a very solemn-looking dog, particularly when he was asleep.

Beyond the window the rain fell, straight down; all that could be seen through it was the deepened green of leaves.

Julian jumped out of bed and picked his clothes up from the floor; they had skidded off the horsehair chair, where he had tossed them the night before.

Othello woke up, too, and greeted him with a wide pink yawn.

"Maybe we'll find a fortune today," Julian told him.

His room also had a paneled wainscoting of dark wood. He had, of course, lost no time in tapping each panel, hoping to find one that sounded hollow, but none of them did, or at least not hollow enough. He tapped them again now, though, just to be on the safe side.

"Nope, no good. Come on, Thel; let's go."

Foster was sliding down the banisters slowly, because he didn't wish to bang into Miss McCurdy on the newel post. He had done this once, and Miss McCurdy's dancing foot, daintily raised, had met the back of his head with the force of a hammer; he could still feel the lump. But sliding down slowly was better than not sliding down at all.

"It's *raining*, it's *pouring*, the old man is *snoring!*" sang Foster lustily, as if this were an anthem of great wit and originality. When he dismounted at the end of the banister, he said: "Today I'm going

1 1 1

to get into that suit of armor. I'm going to try to. Will you help me, Jule?"

"I might. After I've hunted for the safe."

But Portia was not interested in hunting for the safe. She was sure it would never be found, and anyway she wanted to explore the attic storeroom.

"All those trunks, Jule, all those boxes! Why, we might find *anything*. And it's just the day for it!"

"It's just the day to hunt for a safe."

"Why don't you compromise?" Mrs. Blake suggested. "Portia can explore the trunks while Julian searches the attic. My great-uncle Grover *always* kept his safe in the attic."

So after breakfast and their household chores were done, Portia and Julian repaired to the top of the house.

It was nice up there. It had a good dry attic smell, and there was coziness and comfort in the sound of rain on the roof. The storeroom seemed larger now; nearly all of the old furniture had been removed: some of it sold to meet expenses, some— most of it—moved downstairs to beautify the house. All that was left were some chairs without seats and a secretary that had lost its two left legs and leaned like the Tower of Pisa.

The trunks were grouped together in a surrounding of pitchers and basins and other oddments. The dressmaker's dummy stood sentry-duty at one side.

While Portia clattered and clanged, arranging a path amongst the crockery, Julian snooped about under the eaves, opening the doors of washstands. He had to help Portia open the first trunk, and when it was opened, it was a disappointment: nothing but old clothes and a strong smell of camphor. The clothes were petticoats mainly, dozens and dozens of massive petticoats, embroidered and ruffled and ribboned and ruched. There were many vast night-gowns, too, with real lace collars and real lace cuffs; there were pairs and pairs of stockings with embroidered clocks, and pairs and pairs of gloves with pearl buttons, folded in tissue paper. Altogether a very boring trunk, Portia thought. She put all the things back neatly, though. This had been a condition laid down firmly by her mother.

The next trunk was full of furs. Portia gave a faint shriek when she lifted the lid; the last thing she had expected was the sight of fur, and just for an instant she thought an animal was packed in there! It gave her a shock. This trunk released a blinding smell of moth balls and camphor, but the moths had obviously hardened themselves long ago to the defenses laid down against them; they had invaded the trunk as Caesar's legions had invaded Gaul. When Portia lifted out the thick soft cape that lay on top, she gave it a little shake, and all the fur departed from the skins; it rose in clouds of soft black thistledown, tickling her nose and getting in her eyelashes and nestling gently on her arms.

"Ow, Jule, help! Oh, how horrid! Ugh!" Portia blew fur from her lips, brushed herself off, shivered. "I bet this is exactly how Pandora felt!"

"Better keep on digging, then. Hope was in that box, remember? Maybe there's something great in this one, too."

"I'll never know," Portia said, shutting the clasps firmly, still shaking herself, and blowing at the little hairs of fur.

"Do you suppose Mrs. Brace-Gideon ever threw *anything* away?"

"I'm glad she didn't. I like finding things," Julian said. He was wearing a very old pith helmet that sat down on his ears like a soup tureen. Lacking panels to tap and quickly exhausting the safe-searching possibilities of the attic, he had been opening a box or two himself.

In the next trunk that Portia tackled there were many flannel bags with ribbon drawstrings, and each bag contained a pair of shoes or slippers: little pointy shoes with heels, buttoned ones, buckled ones, silk ones with bead-embroidered toes.

"Mrs. Brace-Gideon must have had very tiny feet for such a great big lady," Portia said thoughtfully, looking at the small frayed slipper in her hand.

"Jule?"

"M-m? . . . Yes?"

"Do you think it's really all right for us to do this? I mean, to go through all her very own things like this? *I* don't believe she'd like it if she knew . . . do you?"

Julian considered.

"Well, think of it this way. Mrs. Brace-Gideon has been gone a long, long time. Long before our fathers and mothers were born, even. So now she's like someone in a book, or in history. If we were a couple of archaeologists digging up a buried palace that had belonged to an ancient queen or something, we wouldn't feel wrong about it, would we?"

"No, I suppose not."

"Well, there you are," Julian said handily, and Portia felt better.

Among the large trunks there was a very small one, a box really, covered with cowhide and bearing on its curved lid the initial D, made of brass nail-heads. She lifted the lid cautiously (she had been very cautious since opening the fur trunk) and saw that the little chest was filled to the brim with yellowed paper bundles.

"Jule, come here; let's see what these are."

The paper was so old that it crumbled and powdered when she opened the first bundle; and what it had contained was a seashell, curved and dappled as a little quail.

"Why, how pretty!"

"Look, it's got a label on it, too."

And so it had; a tiny glued-on label with the Latin name of the shell written on it in meticulous old-fashioned handwriting.

"*Cypraea zebra,*" Julian read, pronouncing the *zebra* part correctly.

Portia had opened another bundle and held out a brown shell, fancy as a fern.

"*Murex palmarosae,*" read Julian, stabbing wildly at pronunciation.

Then he undid a bundle himself.

"Anyway, I know what this one is," he said, showing her a large ear-shaped shell, lined with the luminous greens and blues of peacock feathers. "It's an abalone. But that's not what it *says* it is; it says it's a *Haliotis* something or other. I give up. I can't wait till I study Latin. How are you going to be a scientist without it?"

"I don't look forward to it in the least," said Portia. "And I'm never going to be a scientist."

Happy and absorbed, they sat cross-legged on the floor, taking out bundle after bundle. Outside of a museum they had never seen such shells: they were shaped like fans, lockets, towers, pinwheels, hearts, trumpets. They were pleated and patterned, tinted with pink, rose, crimson, yellow, mother-of-pearl; there were several pairs that looked as if they had petals and that were colored like dahlias.

"I'm going to take these down to show Mother, later," Portia said. "This is as good as a Christmas stocking, isn't it, Jule?"

"Better. More in it. I wonder who collected them all and marked them all?"

"There's an initial on the lid: the letter D."

"Oh. Then obviously it must have been that ancestor of Mrs. Brace-Gideon's: that Captain Deuteronomy Dadware. He must have sailed to every beach on earth!"

"The lucky!"

"I know," agreed Julian.

When they were done with the shells, they found some cardboard boxes containing quantities of old, old magazines: fashion magazines of the early 1900s adorned with many pictures of strangely shaped young ladies wearing hairdos that jutted forward from their heads, and large upturned hats that shot forward from the hairdos, so that each young lady looked something like a water pitcher.

Julian soon tired of these, but Portia was entranced. There were other sorts of magazines, too, even older: in one, Portia found a story called *Peter Ibbetson*. She liked the illustrations, and there were children in them, so she began to read . . .

When Foster started calling Julian at the top of his lungs, she hardly heard him, and when Julian told her he was going downstairs, she did not hear him, either. Sometimes a story can open a world for you: you step into it and forget the real one that you live in. Evidently this was such a story.

Foster was waiting on the downstairs landing by the suit of armor. He had a monkey wrench, a pair of pliers, and a can opener.

"I thought maybe you'd need these."

Julian looked at the suit of armor, then at Foster.

"Listen, Fang, it's still too big for you. No use even trying."

"I was afraid so. I suppose I'll just have to wait to grow into it, then, won't I?" said Foster philosophically.

"Perhaps we can try the helmet on you, though. If I can ever get it off; it probably hasn't *been* off in hundreds of years."

Julian gave a mighty tug, and the helmet flew up in his hands with no effort at all.

"Why, it's not even fastened down! O.K., Foss, stand still; let's try this bonnet on you."

Julian lowered the helmet gently down over Foster's head.

"There you go, Sir Launcelot! Can you see all right?"

"Yes, through the eye windows, but it isn't very comfortable in here," Foster complained. His voice inside the helmet had a clangorous twang: a robot's voice. "I don't like it very much. Something keeps tickling my nose. Ow."

"Wait a minute."

Julian lifted the sharp-snouted visor without any trouble. Foster's eyes and nose looked out, and a scrap of paper fluttered to the floor.

"Was that what was bothering my nose?"

But Julian didn't answer him. He had stooped to retrieve the piece of paper and was studying it.

"Now what the—" he muttered, perplexed. Then all at once he jumped straight up in the air as though he had stepped on a bee barefoot. "Oh, man! Oh man, oh *brother!* PORSH!"

And he went thundering up the stairs in a one-boy stampede to the attic.

"Hey, wait!" cried Foster in his robot voice: the steel visor had dropped down again. "Let me out of this thing!"

But Julian was gone. Foster sighed an echoing sigh within the helmet. He could see pretty well through the eye slits, but he felt top-heavy, as though he were wearing an iron bucket on his head, and he couldn't get it off by himself. Sighing again, he felt for the banister and started cautiously up the stairs to find his cousin.

"*Portia!*" roared Julian.

"Now what?" she said, marking her place on the page with her finger.

"Listen to this, just listen! This piece of paper fell out of the helmet—"

"What helmet?"

"Oh, never mind, it doesn't matter. Listen; here's what it says: zero dash, six R dash, two L dash, eight R dash, three whole turns R to eight."

Portia stared at him. "Are you crazy or something?"

"Doesn't it mean anything to you? Listen again. R means right and L means left, see? So it's zero dash, six *right* dash, two *left* dash, eight *right* dash, three whole turns *right* to *eight*. Do you dig it now?"

"No," Portia said.

"Oh, for Pete's sake. It's a combin*ation*, brain. It's sort of a recipe for opening a safe. Now do you see?"

"Mrs. Brace-Gideon's safe?"

Julian just sighed.

"Well, how do you know that's what it is? Maybe it's a recipe for some kind of dance: turn three times to the right and then six times to the left or whatever it is. It *could* be a dance."

Julian rolled his eyes upward.

"How do you start a dance at zero?" he inquired. "Just give me a clue."

At this moment, staring beyond him, Portia gasped. Footsteps were sounding slowly on the attic stairs, and just above the level of the attic floor appeared the helmet of an armored knight.

"Oh, Jule, oh, Jule," she whispered, grasping his arm; and then she wished she hadn't. How she wished she hadn't! Because below the shining head-dress of Sir Launcelot was the figure of her brother Foster, sloppily attired in blue jeans and a grass-stained T-shirt.

"*When Knighthood Was in Flower,*" commented Julian, kindly ignoring his cousin's moment of panic.

"Get me out of here, will you?" begged Foster, his plea reverberating in the helmet. "Please hurry up."

When Julian had liberated him, he did a little hopping.

"Now my head feels light again. I feel light all over, and nice. But you know what, Jule? I bet they used to have a lot of headaches in knight-days. And stiff necks, too. And if their ear itched, how could they ever scratch it?"

10

The Rescue Shell

"What I don't see," Portia objected later that day, "is what's so wonderful about finding the combination when you haven't found the safe and maybe never will."

"I don't know myself, to tell you the truth. It's just that it makes the safe seem *realer*—as if we really would find it. I know that doesn't make sense and it's a dumb way to reason; I guess you'd call it a superstition or a hunch or something, but that's the way I feel."

"It will probably be empty if we do find it, just as Aunt Minnehaha said."

"Maybe," Julian conceded, but he did not sound convinced. He refused to give up the lovely thought of treasure—though for an instant he glimpsed the idea that even if they did find the safe and even if it did contain marvels, it still wouldn't be quite as good as thinking about it and looking for it.

He and Portia were tramping along the soaked drive toward the road to Gone-Away. The rain had stopped, but one felt it had only taken the time to draw a breath or two before it began again. The clouds hung low and wet, and when the small breeze stirred, every tree shook water down.

"I like this day," Julian said. "But I don't see why I do."

The woods looked mysterious and dark, particularly where the honeysuckle had woven its canopies among the branches; the roadside was edged thickly with the green umbrellas of May-apple leaves; and here and there, like a queer bell with a clapper, stood a jack-in-the-pulpit, lonely and alert.

"Indians used to make flour from the roots of those, Aunt Minnehaha says," Portia told Julian. "She said she tried it once and it tasted terrible. She knows absolutely everything about everything that grows: all the plants that you can eat or make medicine of, and all the plants that can make you sick or kill you."

"Well, *I* know that," Julian said. He had eaten many oddities at Aunt Minnehaha's table; some he had liked: the daylily buds dipped in batter and fried, the salads made of young purslane and nasturtium leaves; and some he had not: the pigweed spinach, and the boiled milkweed sprouts.

"Aunt Minnehaha says there's no excuse for any-body starving in this region. Why, you can even eat reindeer moss if you boil it! Did you know that?"

"Well, I'm never going to do it till I have to," Julian said.

He and Portia were bearing gifts for Mrs. Cheever and her brother. Julian had a pound of butter because the old people relished it and had it rarely. Portia was bringing one of Captain Dadware's sea-shells (*Voluta imperialis* was what the label said it was), because Mrs. Cheever had once told her she was "partial to shells."

They came out of the woods and approached the Gone-Away houses. The wet, tall grass was speckled with buttercups, and the air was darting with Judge Chater's swallows, uttering shrill cries of alarm.

At Mrs. Cheever's house a loudly singing radio voice was silenced in mid-warble at their knock. Trip-trip-trip came Mrs. Cheever's rapid footsteps. The door opened.

"Come in, come in," she told them. "We'll hang your waterproofs right here in the entry. What in-

clement weather! But the swamp likes it; I declare you can almost hear it purring!"

Mr. Payton, in the kitchen, rose as they entered, wreathed in pipe smoke.

"Figure of speech. What you can really hear is the frogs," he said. "Good afternoon, Philosophers; it's a pleasure to see bright faces on a dull day. Sit down, do. My sister is making tea."

"I brought some butter for a present." Julian planked the package on the table.

"Wonderful. Thank you; then we'll certainly have toast."

When they were all seated, Portia said: "I brought a present, too, Aunt Minnehaha."

Mrs. Cheever opened the package eagerly. *Voluta imperialis* was a lovely thing: buff, tinged with pink. It was gracefully turned, and on top of it there was a circle of little points that gave it a crowned look.

Mrs. Cheever was enchanted. She clasped her thin hands, and the wintry pink came into her cheeks.

"Oh, Portia, what a beautiful shell! I can't tell you how it pleases me. No, indeed I can't."

She lifted it to her ear, listening, looking thoughtful, looking far away. She smiled to herself.

"Once a seashell saved my life," she said. "At least I think it did."

"Tell!" demanded Portia.

"*Please*," Julian added severely.

"Yes, *please*."

"I never saw the ocean as a child, you know. I never saw any kind of salt water. We lived in town all winter, and in the summer we were always here at Tarrigo (as it was called then), and we asked nothing better.

"Now, the summer I was eleven years old—just your age, Portia—"

"Except I'm eleven-and-a-half," Portia reminded her.

"Yes, well, *almost* your age—I came down with typhoid fever. I know how I got it, too, though no one else did, except for Baby-Belle Tuckertown.

"*That* summer a terrible thing happened to Baby-Belle; a governess was engaged to take care of her! A French governess called Mamzelle. (We children thought that was her real name: 'Mamzelle,' just like 'Edith' or 'Alice' or 'Ethel.') She was a short-tempered woman, spare and tall, with an oblong nose, rather red, and cheekbones that looked varnished. She wore glasses attached to a chain, and she never took her eyes off Baby-Belle. Oh, Baby-Belle was just like a bird in a cage! I felt sorry for her, yes, indeed I did. And besides it was no fun to be with her anymore because Mamzelle was always there, too.

"Poor Baby-Belle! She had always been a free,

happy, willful girl: a regular tomboy, full of ginger! She could throw a ball as well as a boy (almost). She could climb trees like a wild ape of the jungle and swim like a fish! *She* didn't care if her garter broke and her stocking went shriveling down her leg. *She* didn't care if she lost her hair ribbon. I declare, by the end of summer Tarrigo was littered with Baby-Belle's lost hair ribbons! . . . She didn't show one single solitary sign that she would ever grow up to be a young lady. No, indeed she did not.

"So I suppose all that worried her dainty little mother—Mrs. Tuckertown was very small and dainty—but it was Mrs. *Tuckertown's* mother, that bossy old Mrs. Ravenel, who was responsible for hiring Mamzelle, I'll be bound.

"I don't know which was the more miserable: Baby-Belle or that governess. *She* had a perfect horror of the lake. Every time Baby-Belle went swimming, Mamzelle would hover and flap along the shore shrieking and calling: '*Bébé-Belle, Bébé-Belle! Trop loin! Trop loin! Viens ici! Vitement! Immédiatement!*' (That means 'Come here this minute' in French.)

"And then if it rained, poor Baby-Belle, who loved to go barefoot, was made to wear rubbers and carry an umbrella! Oh, the blow to her pride! And when she rode horseback, she had to ride side-saddle; and in the mornings she had to sit still while

Mamzelle curled her hair in long curls around a wet stick, and whenever she talked back or was naughty, Mamzelle would strike her sharply on the knuckles with that same stick.

" 'Oh, I *hate* Mamzelle!' Baby-Belle said to me on one of the few occasions when we were by ourselves. She was ready to cry with rage. 'I'd like to *kill* her!'

"And I said: 'Oh, no, Baby-Belle, you must never hate *anybody* that much!' I was a dreadfully goody-goody child in those days (but I got over it, thank fortune).

"And Baby-Belle stuck her tongue out at me and said: 'I don't give a hang. I hate her, I hate her, I *hate* her! I wish she was dead. So there!'

"Well, the last straw was what happened next.

"Baby-Belle had a dear little dog, a toy fox terrier named Snippet. She thought the world of that little dog and he thought the world of her. He followed her everywhere, and his basket was in her room, though where he really slept, of course, was right on the foot of her bed.

"So one day Baby-Belle did something particularly outrageous. I don't recollect what it was now, but it must have been pretty bad, because that night, to punish her, Mamzelle shut Snippet outside; not just outside Baby-Belle's room, mind you, but outside the *house*.

"Oh, Baby-Belle really did cry then and promised to be good as gold for the rest of her natural life. But to no avail; Mamzelle was relentless. Baby-Belle could hear her poor little dog crying and yelping, but when she attempted to steal downstairs and let him in, she got no farther than her bedroom door, because right out there in the hall Mamzelle was sitting with that stick in her hand! Baby-Belle just had to go back to bed and cry herself to sleep.

"Now late that night a storm came up; a heavy, cold rain. If she hadn't been asleep, I'm sure even Mamzelle would have taken pity on poor Snip and let him in. In the morning when they *did* let him in, he was soaked to the bone and shivering dreadfully. Poor little mite, the next thing anyone knew he was down with pneumonia and had to be taken to Dr. Clisbee, the veterinary, and Dr. Clisbee said he didn't think he could save him—"

"But did he? Could he?" Portia interrupted with great anxiety.

"Yes, dear, in the end he did. Snippet lived to be very old and spoiled and fat. But of course there was no way Baby-Belle could know that at the time. When she thought he was going to die and she'd never see him again, she came racing over to our house and rushed up to my room and told me the whole story with tears running down her cheeks.

"Well, I was perfectly horrified. Yes, indeed I

was, and I said to Baby-Belle: 'Baby-Belle, I agree with you now. I hate Mamzelle, too. I just *hate* her! How'd she let you come here now without her?'

"And Baby-Belle said: 'She thinks I'm in the bathroom. That's the only place she lets me be alone. The amount of time I've spent in our *bathroom* this summer!' And then Baby-Belle told me she had determined to run away. I must never tell a soul, she said, and could I please let her have some money, as she didn't have a cent.

"Well, I had a little bank, and we managed to get the money out of the slit with the aid of a nail file: not much more than a dollar, but that seemed like a good sum to us, then. I told Baby-Belle that I thought she was very wise to run away and that I would get some food for her to take and accompany her part of the way.

"So I got some bread and cheese and cold biscuits from the larder—it was all I could manage; the cook was in the kitchen—and pretty soon we started out, sneaking off into the woods behind Tarrigo so nobody would see us . . .

"We kept turning our heads and looking back, half expecting to see Mamzelle bearing down on us, waving that horrid stick! But we never did, thank fortune, and after a while we knew we were safe and slowed our pace.

"Oh, we walked and we walked. We climbed

fences and crossed meadows, and the sun grew hot and I grew thirsty. It was August, as I recollect: a fine bright day.

"But I grew more and more thirsty. It became positive torture. Finally, I declare I could not stand it, no, I could not, and when we came to a little brook trickling through a meadow, I lay right down on my stomach and lapped up water like a dog. Now, I knew better than that. Papa had told all of us, time and time again, *never* to drink from brooks we didn't know about. But I felt perished with thirst, and I just plain didn't care. No, indeed I did not.

"Pretty soon after that I had to say good-bye to Baby-Belle. 'I'm not the one who's running away,' I told her. 'And I have to go home to lunch.'

"So we said our good-byes, and I wished Baby-Belle good luck. Once I turned around, I remember, and looked at her trudging away, with her hair ribbon untied and dangling as usual and the bag of bread and cheese in her hand, and I wondered when I would ever see her again!

"Well, as matters turned out, I saw her again that very same day. Poor Baby-Belle! She got tired of climbing fences and jumping ditches, and in one field she was chased by a bull; so when she came to the highway, she determined to walk on it for a while. And no *sooner* had she started to do this than along came—who do you think?—Mrs. Brace-

Gideon in her big, glittering barouche with its two big, glittering horses and the coachman and footman on the box.

"Baby-Belle tried to scrunch herself invisible, she told me later, but oh, no, Mrs. Brace-Gideon spotted her with her bright, bold eagle eye and commanded the coachman to stop.

" 'Why, Baby-Belle Tuckertown, what are you doing so far from home?' Mrs. Brace-Gideon asked her. 'And all by yourself, too; why that's not proper! Climb right in, child; we will drive you home at once!'

"Of course, Baby-Belle couldn't think of any way *not* to climb in, so she had to. And it's my suspicion that she was greatly relieved. Running away from home is not the easy thing they claim it is in books. No, indeed it is not."

"Was it the brook water that gave you typhoid?" Julian asked.

"I'm very sure it was. Shortly afterwards, I began to feel ill and listless, and then *very* ill, oh, dreadful, and it seemed to go on and on. . . . So there I was lying on my bed one day, burning up with fever— I was alone in the room for a few minutes for some reason—when I heard a strange sound at the window and there was Baby-Belle flinging her leg over the sill. . . . My room was on the second floor, but I didn't think about that; my fever gave me so many queer thoughts and dreams that nothing seemed queerer than anything else.

" 'Min?' Baby-Belle whispered to me, and I said: 'You better go away quick; I'm catching!' And Baby-Belle said: 'Pshaw, I don't give a hang. I've brought you that seashell Uncle Ninian gave me; the one you always liked, remember? Here, take it.'

"Well, at that moment I didn't really want the shell or anything else—except to be lying in a snow field at the North Pole maybe—but when she pushed it into my hand, it did feel cool, oh, how cool it felt, and I thanked her. Then we heard footsteps in the hall and Baby-Belle skedaddled out the window. (She had borrowed the painter's ladder.)

"I *had* always admired the shell: a beautiful thing, exquisite in color, and smoothly shaped, like an egg. Baby-Belle told me how her Uncle Ninian had visited the Pacific isles; and once when he was in a boat on some lagoon, he had looked down into the water, down and down, and the water was as clear as if it wasn't there at all. The fishes might have been floating in air, Baby-Belle said he said, and they were all colors: gold and blue and purple and striped; and there were sea ferns and things, and way down, below the fishes and the ferns, was this beautiful shell. So Baby-Belle's Uncle Ninian decided to dive down and get it for his niece, and he did, though the water was much deeper than he'd thought, and he felt his lungs would burst before he regained the surface. When he gave the shell to Baby-Belle, he told her that if she held it to her ear, she would hear exactly the way the surf sounded on the barrier reef beyond the lagoon.

"After a while I put the shell to my own ear, and sure enough it seemed as if I could really hear the soft roar of surf on a distant reef; and when my dreams began again, they were all about the cool, clear water of the lagoon and the fishes drifting and the sea ferns waving, and I really believe, I really do, that that shell and the dreams it gave me helped me to recover."

"Minnie, you never told me that story before," said Mr. Payton rather indignantly, as he knocked the ashes from his pipe. "Nobody could ever figure out how you'd got typhoid—ever. Not even Papa."

"Oh, I still have a few secrets up my sleeve," replied Mrs. Cheever airily. "And the story isn't quite ended, because when I was convalescing, Baby-Belle came to see me. My hair had been cut off short as a boy's—they did that in those days when you had a bad fever—and Baby-Belle was really envious. She resented the poor judgment Fate had shown in making her a girl instead of a boy in the first place.

"She picked up the shell—I kept it on my bed-side table—and she said: 'You know why I gave you this, Min? I gave it to you because Mamzelle is gone. She's *gone!* Forever! And it's all because of you!'

" 'Me?' I said, perfectly bewildered, and Baby-Belle said: 'Yes. Because when Mamzelle heard you had typhoid fever, she flew into a panic, she was so scared she'd catch it. Why, she couldn't get away fast enough, and she packed in such a rush that there was a long black stocking hanging out of one end of her suitcase like a tail!'

"So we both laughed at that picture, and then Baby-Belle looked sort of worried and she said: 'You know something, Min? When Mamzelle said she was leaving, I couldn't help feeling glad as anything that you'd caught typhoid fever! But only because it chased *her* away, though, Min; *you* know that. . . . But I felt so bad about feeling glad that I thought I'd better give you Uncle Ninian's shell that you always admired so. Then I knew I'd feel all right again. And I did.'

"And that *is* the end of the story," Mrs. Cheever said decisively.

"But what about the shell, Aunt Minnehaha?" Portia asked her. "Where is it? Have you got it still? I'd love to see it."

A strange little expression flitted over Mrs. Cheever's face.

"No," she said. "No, as a matter of fact, I no longer have it." She hesitated a moment, then went on. "The shell proved to be extremely rare, and after the death of my husband, Mr. Cheever, when I fell upon hard times, I sold it. The amount I received for it tided me over until I could return to Tarrigo—or Gone-Away, as it was called by then. So it was twice that that seashell came to my rescue! I hope it has been as kind to those who purchased it."

"But I wish you had it still." Portia sighed. Money seemed to her a very troubling, grown-up thing.

Outside, the rain was pouring down again, pouring hard. It trounced the leaves and bounced from the sills. Mrs. Cheever's hens, complaining, scurried for shelter; but the duck waddled serenely along the path. Now and then he would stop and look about him, and one could have sworn that he was smiling.

"We'd better go," said Julian.

"Would you like me to drive you?" offered Mr. Payton.

But, no, they wanted to run home. This rain was exciting; a massive downpour, and massive, too, was the sound of the summer's first thunder. It had a rolling, good-natured quality, like the roar of a well-fed lion.

"Good-bye, Aunt Minnehaha, good-bye, Uncle Pin!"

And Portia and Julian burst from the house, leaping and shouting: glad that it was raining hard and glad that they were children.

11

The Hot Spell

Early in July the weather turned very hot.

"Ain't had a spell like this in fourteen years," Eli Scaynes said happily, for though wiry, he was thin and elderly. The heat just suited his bones, and he went about his work humming a tuneless tune.

It suited the children, too, who wore as little as possible in the way of clothing and walked in and out of the hose sprinkler whenever they wanted to. It was hot in the morning when they woke up, and it kept on growing hotter all day long: still, burning, intense. The windless evenings, sparked with the drifting lights of fireflies and the fixed lights of stars, were so warm that the children were allowed to stay up later than usual. They made firefly lanterns and carried them off in the shadows, glimmering like will-o'-the-wisps, while the grownups sat in the lawn chairs talking and tinkling the ice in their cool glasses.

Each day it was hotter. Julian and Portia felt proud of it.

"The thermometer says 95°," Julian announced one morning; and on the next he said triumphantly, "It's 98!"

And then one day it was 100°, and the children were overjoyed, though the grownups were not.

The sun-beaten roses opened wide, large as lettuces, dropping their petals all too soon; and the soft new grass of the lawns felt warm and wilted under a bare foot.

The grownups sighed and complained; the dogs hung their tongues out; and the new kitten, Mousenick, slept flat as a dead kitten in any scrap of shade.

Mr. Ormond Horton had been as good as his word; he had brought Portia one of his cat's best kittens. He (it was a he-kitten) was little and gray, with tabby stripes on his sides like the wavery marks on watered silk, and eyes that were still blue because he was so young.

He did all the things a proper kitten should do. He romped, rolled, pursued his tail delightfully, tapped at a thimble with his perfect paw. He could flatten his ears, crouch, growl and stalk like a tiger. He could purr a miniature purr and wash his face better than Foster could. At dusk, small though he was, he could be quite alarming as he humped his back up, bushed his tail, and danced sideways staring eerily at something no one else could see.

Julian had named him, though Portia had planned to. He had just scooped the kitten up in his hand and said: "Here you go, Mousenick," and the name had stuck.

Everybody in the family liked him, and Gulliver and Othello did not mind him. As for Portia, whenever she looked at him, her heart melted.

During those hot days the Gone-Away houses stood cooking in the sun, giving off a smell of baked wood and dry rot, and very, very faintly of creosote: a delicious smell, the children thought. In the burning heat they were sometimes lured into the shady interiors of the most neglected houses, where, if they penetrated deeply enough, climbing over the rubble, the broken galleries and stairways, they could usually find a place, an inner hall or pantry, that was cool.

Judge Chater's was such a house; at the heart of the debris his dark-paneled dining room was like a cave: so damp that toadstools grew between the floorboards and the walls were stippled with mildew. Vandals had scratched their names on the plaster, broken the windowpanes and the Tiffany glass shades of the wall fixtures. Rainbow-colored shards glimmered among the toadstools.

"Yes. It's cool, but it's creepy," Portia said to Julian, who had led her there. "I don't—I'm not sure I like it."

"Well, it's not anyplace you'd want to stay," Julian admitted; and both of them thought of what Mrs. Cheever had told them.

"Next to Mrs. Brace-Gideon's house, the judge's house was the grandest one at Tarrigo," she had said. "Full of painted screens, you know, and jade figurines and porcelain vases, because he had spent many years in the Orient. He was a widower: a very rich elderly gentleman with no family left, except for his servants. They were all Chinese. I remember how they used to sound talking together: quacking and singing, or that's how it sounded to *us*. They were very nice and they liked children. It was so long ago that each of the menservants still wore a pigtail; and the women wore little coats and trousers, and when they ran, they trotted. All of them trotted on their boat-shaped slippers. . . .

"Sometimes, I declare, even now when the wind's from the northeast, I fancy it carries a memory of their voices, a very faint quacking and singing!"

Standing in the cool ruin, Portia said to Julian: "I know I'd die if I should ever meet a ghost, but if I met a Chinese ghost, I'd die *more!*"

At that moment a swallow flew in through a window, swished like a scimitar past their faces, uttered its frightened chatter, and departed as Portia uttered a frightened squeak.

"Julian, come on; let's *go!*"

"Take it easy, now, ta-a-ke it easy," Julian drawled; but he was glad to go himself.

On the day the thermometer showed one hundred degrees, Portia and Julian set out early for Gone-Away. It was only a little after nine, but already every trace of dew was licked away. As usual they carried their lunch boxes, but for a change each was wearing a straw hat. The sun's rays could be brutal as the day neared noon.

They had to stop to watch a chipmunk in the woods; they had to stop while Julian caught a butterfly; when they heard a cuckoo's wooden-mallet note, they had to stop until Julian could spot him with the field glasses.

At Gone-Away, wading through yarrow and Queen Anne's lace, they made straight for Mr. Payton's house and found him working in his garden. He had a tropical, exotic look because he was wearing the pith helmet Julian had discovered in the attic. They had decided to give this to him when they noticed how often, on these hot days, he would remove his broad-brimmed hat, sighing as he blotted his forehead with one of his fine frayed handkerchiefs. The present had pleased him greatly.

"Always, since boyhood, I have longed to own a solar topee!" he exclaimed.

"That's another name for a pith helmet," Julian murmured to Portia, and Portia said she knew it.

Mr. Payton turned the helmet on his hand, admiring it. Then he clapped it on his head, slightly tilted, stroked his mustache preeningly, and went to look at his reflection in a windowpane.

"Now, all I need is a large umbrella with a green lining. And a camel," he had said. "Oh, and perhaps a pyramid or a sphinx. But seriously, Philosophers, this topee will be a boon: light and cool, yet no bee's sting can penetrate it when I tend the hives."

And after that whenever he *did* tend his beehives, whether the weather was warm or cold, he always wore the pith helmet under the bee veil instead of his usual hat.

Now he doffed it to them.

"Good morning, Philosophers. A pleasure to see you. We're in for another scorcher, I fear."

"The thermometer says 100° right now," Julian was glad to inform him. "*Already*. It will be worse than that by noon!" He sounded perfectly delighted, and was.

"By Jupiter!" Mr. Payton gave a whistle and dropped his hoe on the ground. "This is no day for gardening, then. Perhaps we'd better go and see how my sister is faring, though she never seems bothered by the heat."

They found Mrs. Cheever sitting on her front porch quite contented. Tarrigo lay at her feet, panting. He rolled his eyes at them pathetically, too hot to bark; but Mrs. Cheever looked cool and composed. She was wearing a dress of embroidered India mull. Once it had been white—"My sister Persy's graduation dress, just fancy!"—but time had tanned it and frayed it in many places. It looked very pretty, though, and she had pinned a rose to her collar, and the bow on her hair was the same color as the rose. She was sitting in a rocking chair with her mending, and on the table beside her lay a palm-leaf fan with green words painted on it: Atlantic City, 1889.

"Why, children, your clubhouse will be suffocating, won't it?"

"We're not going to use it today," Julian told her. "The guys—the other fellows—Tom Parks and Joe Felder are coming here to meet us—"

"And Lucy Lapham, too," Portia interrupted. "She's back visiting the Gaysons, thank goodness."

"The membership reunited, eh?" said Mr. Payton.

"Yes. They'll be here at eleven, and then we'll decide what to do. I wish there was anything to swim in but the brook."

"They won't let us use the river; too dangerous," Portia explained dolefully. "Oh, if only Tarrigo could turn back into a lake just for one day! I'm *dying* for a swim."

"Now, wait a moment, wait a moment," said Mr. Payton, frowning. "Let me see. There used to be— oh, years ago—but there *used* to be a limestone quarry back in the woods above Pork Ferry. *Way* back. Abandoned. Springs fed into it. Cold. Refreshing. Wonder if it's still there? Probably not. Probably a used-car lot by now, or a public dump, or a drive-in motion-picture theater, or some other confounded thing," he concluded grumpily; the heat had made him grumpy.

"But we could go and see, couldn't we, sir? If you gave us directions."

"Nonsense, I'll drive you there in the Machine. As far as I *can*; after that we'll walk."

"Now, Pin, I wonder if you should," his sister objected. "It might be too much for you. You might get heat exhaustion."

"Perfect nonsense, Minnie. You make me feel like an old crock!"

"Very well, then. Very well." Mrs. Cheever

creaked her rocker back and forth. "How I wish you would not call me Minnie!"

Portia fanned herself with her hat. "We went exploring in Judge Chater's house yesterday, Aunt Minnehaha. I didn't like it very much. I thought it was spooky."

"I suppose it may be, now, all broken as it is. It was very grand once, though, wasn't it, Pin? . . . And every summer, just about this time of year, Judge Chater would give an evening party. He invited all the Tarrigo grownups and other ones from Pork Ferry and even Creston.

"Oh, we children hung out of our windows on that night! We could just glimpse the Chinese lanterns in the garden: big pearls, they looked like! And we could hear the carriages come driving up, so festive-sounding, and then the greetings and gabblings and the ladies laughing and trilling; and from the back of the house, where the kitchen was, came the sing-songing of the Chinese people. And the smell that wafted toward us! The party smell! Oh, Pin, do you remember?"

"Chinese delicacies. Fine cigars. Perfumery," Mr. Payton said with relish, stroking his mustache reminiscently.

"And there was a noise of popping, just like my little brother Lex's popgun, but it was really bottle corks. And then always at one point a silence would fall; an important chord would be struck on the piano, an introduction played, and *then* Mrs. Brace-Gideon's great big singing voice would come ballooning out of the windows into the night . . . into the summer night . . . and we children would hold our ears and roll up our eyes and groan out loud. . . ."

"It was generally opined that Mrs. Brace-Gideon had her cap set for Judge Chater," Mr. Payton said.

"But she never got him. No, indeed she did not!" Mrs. Cheever shook her head decisively.

"The best thing, though," she continued, "the thing we were all waiting for, groggy with sleep though we were, was that very late in the evening —oh, very late indeed—a display of fireworks would be set off at the end of Judge Chater's dock."

"Set off by Wing Pin and Fat Lo, my two good friends," said Mr. Payton.

"And what fireworks they were! Weren't they, Pin? Oh, I never saw anything to equal them! Dragons! Fountains! Flower gardens! Big blazing birds! All made of fiery stars and colors! And everything sizzled and banged and dazzled, and there was a wonderful, exciting, Chinese-y, burning smell. Wasn't there, Pin?"

"M-m-m!" agreed her brother, smiling as he remembered. "Yes . . . yes . . . Wing Pin and Fat Lo. Years since I've thought of them. Fine fellows.

One fat, one thin. (Fat Lo was the thin one.) They kept Tark and me and all the rest of the Tarrigo rascals supplied with Chinese firecrackers. Not just for the Fourth of July. No. All the time. Kept us very happy. Not the girls, though."

"Not the grownups, either," said his sister. "Poor Mrs. Ravenel—"

But Mrs. Cheever was interrupted here by the arrival of the other charter members of the Philosophers' Club: plump Tom Parks, handsome Joe Felder, and Portia's special friend Lucy Lapham, a dark-eyed girl with curly hair.

"Oh, I'm so glad to see you!" cried Portia, giving her a hug. "I'm so glad to see another girl!"

After the flurry of greetings, Tom Parks sat down on the porch steps with a heavy groan.

"I bet I've melted off five pounds."

"Better melt off twenty more," Julian advised him kindly.

They all looked very hot from their long walk. Their cheeks were strawberry red, their noses spangled with sweat, and their hair was soaking.

"I bet you could fry an egg on my hat," Joe Felder said. "I mean it's hot, man, *hot!*"

"Well, cheer up, though." Portia comforted them. "Uncle Pin is going to show us a place to swim."

"*If* it's still there," the old gentleman amended.

"Oh, boy, I hope it is!" Tom said fervently. Then

his face fell. "We didn't bring any bathing suits. Heck!"

But Mrs. Cheever, it seemed, was equal to any occasion. She recalled that in one of the trunks that had been brought from the Big House, she had seen a quantity of ancient bathing suits, all sizes, that had long ago been worn by the Payton children.

"As Portia says, we were a very 'keeping' family. Thank fortune," Mrs. Cheever observed. "Girls, come with me to my storeroom, will you?"

And soon their arms were laden with the old wool bathing suits, smelling of mothballs so strongly that, as Lucy said, "You could lean against it."

"I advise you each to wear a boy's suit," Mrs. Cheever told them. "Good gracious, when I think of what *we* had to wear! Dresses with skirts and collars and sleeves! Stockings and sand shoes! *Hats*, straw hats, tied under our chins! I wonder they didn't make us wear gloves!"

Each boy's suit consisted of a striped tunic and striped trousers.

"It was the fashion then," said Mrs. Cheever. "Stripes were considered very continental."

Packed into the Franklin, Mr. Payton and the children steamed along the road to the hot highway, contributing an unusual odor of mothballs to the day. The highway danced with heat and shimmered with puddle mirages; and once Mr. Payton stopped the car so that they could watch the phenomenon of a turtle hurrying, *trotting*, across the blazing asphalt that burned its feet.

"I never saw a turtle run before. I never knew they could," Julian said in awe.

"They keep their secret well," Mr. Payton agreed. "It occurs to me that that old fable of the tortoise and the hare may well be simply propaganda put out by the hare."

They drove through the red-hot main street of Pork Ferry, where people carrying bags of groceries stopped to gape at the loud, majestic progress of the Franklin. Mr. Payton bowed cordially to left and right, like visiting royalty.

After they left the village and the highway, they drove along a wooded road, slowly ascending. The Franklin huffed and struggled, and all of them, except Mr. Payton, got out and walked to make things easier for it.

"Just about here, I'd say," Mr. Payton announced finally, applying the brake. "There seems to be the remnant of a footpath."

It was a remnant indeed, and they kept losing it. The woods were shady, it was true, but the shade was hot and close; cat-claw scratched at them, and gnats kept trying to get into their eyes.

Mr. Payton, in the lead, fought his way through hazel bushes.

"It's clearing ahead," he called encouragingly, and in a moment they heard him give an exclamation of pleasure.

"Well, by Jove. Just look at that! A sight for sore eyes, Philosophers, and the same, *exactly* the same, as it was more than sixty years ago!"

The quarry held deep water in its cup: a little lake that lay still as a jewel, clear as a jewel, without a breath of air to wrinkle its surface. On this scorching noonday it was indeed a sight for sore eyes.

"Suave," breathed Julian.

"What are we waiting for!" demanded Tom, pulling off his shirt. He and the other boys scrambled into the bushes to put on their suits, and Lucy and Portia found their own little dressing room behind a rock. Soon they were in the striped bathing suits. Lucy giggled at the sight of Portia, and Portia giggled at the sight of Lucy. The tight-fitting trousers reached well below their knees; the tight-fitting tunics hugged their ribs and had high necks and little shoulder sleeves. Lucy's stripes were black and yellow.

"You look like a big fat hornet," Portia said. *Her* stripes were red, white, and blue.

"You look like a skinny little patriotic barber pole," Lucy retorted.

The boys looked just as odd as they did, and so did Mr. Payton, whose suit, also vividly striped, was a relic of the same era.

Good-natured jeers and insults filled the air. So did an alien smell of mothballs. But not for long. Soon the children were popping into the water, happy as frogs.

It was cold! Cold and delicious, and so clear that they could see the carpet of drowned leaves lying far below them on the bottom.

At first they just swam and soaked and luxuriated. The midday sun blazed down on them. Mr. Payton swam the breast stroke holding his beard well out of the water and smiling benignly.

"Ah, by Jupiter, ah, by Jove," he purred contentedly.

"Let's stay here all day long, Uncle Pin, can we? Let's stay until it's suppertime."

"Why not, why not? When we're chilled, we'll lie on the rocks and bake ourselves dry, and then we'll swim again."

After a while Julian, who wanted to show off his diving, managed to find a plank and some boulders, and contrived a springboard. For the first few dives his skill was greatly admired, but then everybody else wanted a turn, even Tom Parks, who slapped the water resoundingly with his stomach every time.

The rock walls of the quarry echoed with squabbles and laughter and splashing and shouts. It echoed often with the words: "Look at me! Watch this! Hey, you guys, watch *me!*"

Old Mathew Partridgeberry, a recluse who lived in a house halfway up the mountain, heard the racket and came to see who was making it. Peeping between hazel leaves, he saw the children in their hornet stripes, and the old man in his. Not since his own distant childhood had he seen bathing suits like these! It gave him a turn. For a moment he felt a chill of superstition: could it be . . . ghosts? A switch in time? . . . But then he smiled to himself. No. These were real live children; live, loud, twentieth-century children. A prank of some sort, or a game, no doubt. Still smiling, he turned away and was lost in the shrubbery, and no one ever knew that he had been there.

12

The Plan

It was a beautiful summer. There was just enough rain to keep the land green and the farmers contented, but most of the days were warm and fair.

The children swam, roamed, rode their bicycles up hill and down dale, picnicked, conducted meetings in the club, and paid visits almost daily to their Gone-Away friends. In the long, light evenings they played Prisoner's Base and Any Over and Allee, Allee, In-Free.

In addition, they had their private projects. Foster and Davey, though they had their own little house on Craneycrow, decided to build themselves another in the boughs of an oak tree on "The Property." They went to work with hammers and nails, inflicting so many minor injuries upon themselves that Julian said the tree house should be named Palazzo Band-Aid. Between hammerings, the little boys could be

heard arguing and conversing, shrill as the sparrows
that clustered in the Boston ivy.

Portia and Lucy practiced ballet (Lucy took lessons in Albany). They had scratched out a garden
for themselves containing only the vegetables they
preferred: tomatoes, lettuce, onions, and carrots.

"No beets!" Portia said firmly.

"No spinach!" said Lucy.

"Oh, no, never! And absolutely no cucumbers
and no broccoli and no cabbages!"

Another project was the rehabilitation of the six
sad little rooms in the attic. Mr. Ormond Horton
donated the paint, but the girls proposed to do the
work themselves.

"Let's have each one a different color," said
Portia. "One blue, one green, one red—or, no,
pink—"

"And one yellow, and one orange, and—what
other colors are there?"

"Purple?" suggested Portia.

"Yes, why not! I never did see a purple room."

Fortunately for them, the rooms were tiny. Even
so, the work was harder than they had supposed,
and nobody would help them. The little boys offered
to hopefully, but were refused.

"You know what *that* would mean," Portia said
darkly.

"Paint *everywhere* but on the walls," said Lucy, sounding like her own grandmother. She had a green streak in her hair that wouldn't wash out, and Portia's fingernails were purple. But it was all in a good cause; the rooms were beginning to look cheerful, to say the least.

Julian had started a paper route that took him half the morning, and the other boys, too, had part-time jobs.

Mr. Blake's vacation was over; he had had to return to his work in the city and only came out for weekends, but his weekend projects were so numerous that, as he said, he had "to get back to the office to relax."

As for Mrs. Blake, she was seldom seen without something in her hands: hammer and nails, or paint and paintbrush, or lengths of fabric. "You really never get finished with a house," she said contentedly. But sometimes she just wandered quietly from room to room, gloating.

The Villa Caprice continued to offer surprises: certain tall spikey plants near the house turned out to be lilies: great freckled fragrant ones. A drawer in the library desk was discovered to be full of jigsaw puzzles, dominoes, playing cards, and a chess set. Some surprises were not so pleasant: the leak that appeared in the dining room; the peculiar temperament of the bathroom plumbing; the fact that the drawing-room fireplace smoked in rainy weather.

Gradually they became familiar with the sounds peculiar to the house: the stair tread in the hall stairs that chirped like a cricket when anyone stepped on it; the swing door into the dining room that whooshed and sighed; the way the chimneys rumbled when the wind was high. All these were nice because they were the sounds of home.

"This place *is* home, now," Portia said. "And the apartment in New York is just the place we stay in in wintertime."

"Winter. Ugh," said Foster. "I wish it wouldn't get here for eleven years."

But the summer, as summers are apt to do, was spinning itself out fast, too fast. Already it was August.

"It's funny," Portia observed. "I never really believe in school in summertime. I know it exists, and all, but it just doesn't seem really *real*."

"Mine does," Lucy said. "I can smell it if I think about it. I can smell the blackboard and the varnish on my desk and the wet floor in the hall when they've scrubbed it."

"I move we change the subject," suggested Tom Parks. "Is there another stuffed egg on the premises?"

They had met, all of them, for a picnic at Gone-Away—both the official groups, of course: the members of the Fang Club, all two of them; the members of the Philosophers' Club, all five.

It was exactly the sort of day for watermelon, so that was what they had for dessert. Foster luxuriated, sinking two thirds of his face into the icy pink slice.

"Hey, you know what, Dave?"

"No, what?"

"My new front teeth are getting to be more than just edges. I can sort of bite with them now."

"I've been biting with mine for months," Davey said wearily.

Except for a watery crunching and slurping, there was silence; then Foster said: "But you know what, Dave?"

"No, what?"

"When we've got our real full-grown front teeth, we won't be able to call it the Fang Club anymore, because we won't have any fangs."

"What will we call it then?"

"I don't know. We'll think of something."

"What about the Dental Maturity Club?" suggested Julian; but of course they didn't pay any attention to *him*.

After the watermelon had been eaten right down

to the rind, the little boys repaired to Craneycrow
and the girls went off to visit Mrs. Cheever.

Tom Parks sighed and let his belt out a notch.
Then he and Julian and Joe, for no particular reason
and not really thinking about it, climbed up in the
Vogelhart willow tree. Sun and food had made them
lazy, and each of them found a perching place and
sat there like a sleepy baboon high among the wind-
sifting, sun-sifting leaves.

Swallows looped and dipped around Judge Chater's tipsy cupola.

"You know something, Jule?" Joe Felder said. "I bet you'd never dare spend a night in one of these old dumps. Judge Chater's house, for instance."

"I bet I would."

"I bet you wouldn't."

"I bet I would," but then Julian, who was a fairly honest boy, felt compelled to add: "Not alone, though. *With* somebody. You, maybe. How about it? I dare you!"

It was a bright, lively afternoon. Foster and Davey could be heard sparrow-chirping on their island, and Mr. Payton, distantly, could be heard whistling in his garden. To the left, there was the scatterbrained conversation of hens and a sound of feminine voices as Mrs. Cheever and the girls came out of her house to go berrying.

The world was a safe place. Anyone could see that it was safe.

"O.K.," Joe said. "You say when."

"You too, Tom?"

"Well, I guess so." Tom agreed, but not with alacrity.

"We'll do it on the night of the full moon," Julian said. "That's only three nights off, Thursday. We'll be able to find our way around better by moonlight, and another thing is—another rule is—that we can't bring any flashlights."

"Heck, why not?"

"That would make it too easy," Julian said happily. His very eyeglasses sparkled with excitement. "We don't just want this to be an *easy* sort of thing, do we? Because it has to be in the nature of a—of a test."

"Why?" Tom wanted to know.

"For discipline," Julian replied. He had a noble feeling in his forehead as he said it. "Self-discipline," he added.

"I don't know if I need it," Tom said. "I *get* discipline. I get it everywhere. I get it at home, I get it at school, I get it in the mornings working at Bilmeyer's store."

"Oh, everybody needs it," Julian assured him. "And listen, you guys, this whole operation has to be kept secret. Absolutely secret. From everyone."

"Our families, even?"

"Especially our families. They might say no."

"From the girls, too?" asked Joe.

Julian just ignored him. That went without saying.

"We'll slip out after dark, see, when everything's quiet. We'll meet here under the tree. I'll be spending the night at the Blakes's so I can get here fast, and you guys will have your bikes . . ."

Busily and happily he laid his plans, and soon his companions were infected with his enthusiasm; even Tom.

"We'll bring some blankets in case we get sleepy," Julian said.

"And some food in case we get hungry," Tom added.

"And an alarm clock to wake us up in time to go home before they miss us. I'll bring it," Joe volunteered.

Thursday came: fine and clear and very warm. Julian smuggled three blankets into Judge Chater's house. He had also brought a bottle of Mrs. Cheever's A.P. Decoction because at night the mosquitoes were apt to be bad. He crawled cautiously up the rickety stairs that swayed and swagged beneath his feet. Reconnoitering, the day before, he had found that there was a fairly sound room on the second floor not quite so littered and ruined as the rest. Besides, though he scarcely admitted it to himself, to be upstairs seemed somehow—safer.

Now in the broad light of day even the hint of such a thought appeared ridiculous. Sunshine blazed beyond the broken windows; flies buzzed in and out. Everything looked perfectly ordinary and cheerful, however shabby.

"Nothing to it," Julian remarked aloud, sweeping fallen plaster aside with his foot and clearing a space to spread the blankets on.

"Hey, Jule," called Tom's voice below stairs. "Where are you anyway?"

"Up here; come on up! Take it easy on the stairs, though."

Tom came, carrying a tin box under his arm. He lifted the lid of it and peered in lovingly.

"Three chocolate-almond bars," he recited. "Three bags of potato chips. Three bags of salted peanuts. And Joe's bringing cold root beer tonight along with the alarm clock."

"Great," Julian said. "And I know where I can get some salami and a bottle of dill pickles."

"M-m," murmured Tom wordlessly. The thought of dill pickles made his mouth water; then he said: "You know, Jule, this doesn't seem like a test, or discipline, or anything. It just seems like a neat thing to do. It just seems like fun."

"I know," said Julian. "Let's hope we feel the same tomorrow morning."

13

The Night of the Full Moon

Julian thought that the Blakes's house would never quiet down that night. He waited in his room, and waited. He felt himself getting sleepy and fought himself awake again. But finally, after all the last good-nights were said, after all the tooth-brushings and murmurings and yawns and the closing of doors, he was able to creep out of his room and inch his way along the hall. Pressed against his chest, he held the bag of salami and dill pickles as if to keep them quiet, too.

Going down the front stairs, he forgot about the chirping stair tread, and of course it chirped loudly. Julian froze against the banister, staring down at Miss McCurdy's dim figure on the newel post. He had chosen to come this way because the back stairs were uncarpeted and noisy, and now— But no one came; nothing happened. Soon he continued down and tiptoed through the dark, watchful house to the back door. Behind him, the kitchen clock ticked in a little scolding voice.

Outdoors the sound of crickets shimmered in the air; everywhere, all over the summer land. The bright moon was small in the sky; it lighted up the edges of the clouds that were swimming toward it. A small soft wind moved forward, and the trees, dry with August, rustled their leaves and whispered.

Julian hurried along the drive. Moon patches dappled the ground, moving now as wind stirred the branches above. The honeysuckle trees were frightening at night; they looked like stooping figures: old soldiers, giants, in great dragging cloaks. Julian would not have admitted to a soul that his heart was hurrying in his chest, but it was. He was glad of the strong, reassuring smell of the salami pressed against his ribs.

He slowed down when he came to the clearing, and his heart slowed down, too. The clearing was blue with moonlight and humming with crickets. The wind was warm. Far to the right there was a lighted window in Mr. Payton's house. Far to the left there was another in Mrs. Cheever's. Julian whistled a tune softly. He felt fine; everything was going right, and there, sure enough, waiting under the willow, was good old Tom Parks.

"Hey, where've you been! You're late!"

"Couldn't help it; they just wouldn't settle down and I had to wait. Where's Joe?"

"Search me. I waited for him, too, but his house was all dark, and when I threw pebbles at his window, they made such a racket I was scared his folks would wake up, so I scrammed out of there pretty fast."

"Well, there's no sense waiting any longer. Let's go in. I don't think he chickened out, do you?"

"No, not Joe. He's no coward."

They entered the gaunt old house on tiptoe. It was still in there, and stale. It smelled of age, of decay, of damp; and it was very dark. The swimming clouds had caught the moon and covered it. Wind was beginning to tease the house.

"Ow!" exclaimed Tom in an outraged whisper; he had barked his shin on something. "I think it was a crazy idea not to bring a flashlight. I think it was dumb. Ow!"

The stairway quivered and swung as the boys felt their way up, and then felt their way to the room they had chosen. The moon tore itself free from clouds just long enough to light them in; then it was seized and darkened again. Far, far away there was a sort of shuddering. One could hardly have called it a sound.

"Was that thunder?" Tom asked apprehensively.

"I don't think so," Julian said. He certainly hoped not. He walked over to one of the windows and leaned his arms on the sill. Mrs. Cheever's house was dark now; all the world was dimmed, but you could tell there was a moon somewhere; the clouds could not quite smother its light. Below, the Vogelhart willow tossed softly in the wind.

"What do you say we have a snack?" Tom suggested.

That seemed a good idea to both of them, and they spread the blankets out on the floor and sat down. Tom rattled open the metal box. Julian crackled open the paper bag. Soon the air was warmed with an odor of peanuts and salami and dill pickle, and there was a sound of crunching. In the darkness everything tasted perfectly delicious.

"But salty," Julian objected. "Do you realize, Tom, that every single thing we brought is salty? Except the chocolate, and that always makes you thirsty anyway."

"Well, we counted on Joe and the root beer. How could we know? I'm not thirsty yet, though, are you? If we don't think about it, maybe we won't be."

"Maybe not." Julian agreed doubtfully. But the

more he tried not to think about it, the more he thought about it. He could feel himself inventing his own thirstiness.

"Doggone it, what do you suppose *happened* to Joe?"

"I don't know. Fell asleep maybe, but there's no use worrying," Tom said philosophically. He was clanging things back into the tin box. "There's plenty left over for a snack later on if we need it."

He yawned a loud, satisfied yawn.

"Maybe we should sleep for a while."

"All right," Julian said, thinking about thirstiness; and they each stretched out on a blanket—it was much too warm for covers—and were quiet for nearly two minutes.

"Ow," Tom complained. "I never knew my bones had so many corners."

"You think *you* have troubles. You've got good natural padding, and I haven't. This is the hardest floor I ever felt."

"Well, we'll just have to get used to it. Soldiers do. Marines do."

"Rugs do," added Julian. "I don't mind the hardness of the floor so much, but I'm getting so thirsty I may have to drink the A.P. Decoction!"

Tom laughed. "Good thing you brought it anyway; here come the mosquitoes."

It was true. Somewhere just above their heads

there was a sound like the wailing of the tiniest violin imaginable. Then another.

Hurriedly, Julian slapped his face and arms with Mrs. Cheever's famous Anti-Pest Decoction and handed the bottle to Tom. The room was suddenly permeated with an extraordinary smell, and because of it the sound of little violins diminished and was gone.

There was another distant shuddering in the air.

"It *is* thunder, Jule," Tom said accusingly. "I told you it was."

"It may never get here, though. It's a long way away."

"It will get here," Tom pronounced gloomily. "Just wait and see."

Outside, the wind was picking up; the trees churned under it, and all the reeds of Gone-Away hissed and rustled as they bowed.

"Sh-h! What's *that!*" whispered Tom, clutching Julian's arm.

"Hey, quit *grabbing* me like that; it startles me. What's *what?*"

"Listen—"

Clap came the sound; then a sort of jiggle and squeak; then *clap* again.

"Oh, that. It's only a broken shutter banging against the house. I think."

"You hope."

Both boys were whispering now, and Julian was wishing that they had chosen a room with a door that would close and preferably lock. This door had been wedged and warped ajar by time and weather. Nothing would ever close it now.

An abandoned house takes the wind the way a ship takes heavy seas. It creaks throughout, seems to stretch and groan, then settle for a bit, then stretch and groan again. It does other things, too, or at least this one did: it had a constantly varying repertory of creaks, tap-taps, and sounds like the most hesitant of footsteps.

When Julian had thought about this adventure, he had imagined that the scary thing would be the deadly silence of Judge Chater's midnight house. But now it was the sounds—all these different sounds—that were scaring him, and in his heart of hearts he was beginning to wish that he had never insisted on this idiotic undertaking: this "test!" The only good thing about it, at the moment, was that he felt too worried to be thirsty.

Evidently Tom shared his attitude about the venture. "I don't know," he said. "I don't see what good it's going to do our characters just to sit here in a thunderstorm in a beat-up old house, feeling scared. I think it's going to be *bad* for our characters. It is for mine."

"Well, why don't you go on home, then? Go ahead."

"And leave you here alone? You know I wouldn't. And anyhow, I'd probably get struck by lightning on my bike."

As if its name had been a cue, a tongue of lightning flickered, bright and close. It lighted the room so that for a split second each boy saw the worried solemn look on the face of the other. Then it was dark again, and approaching thunder slammed in the sky.

The broken shutter banged frantically; the old house strained and shook as if it were trying to tear itself loose from its foundations; and after a while the rain began all at once so that it fell on the roof like a solid thing.

The storm went on and on; they could not guess how long, but they knew when it had reached its pitch. The lightning, blue and blinding, winked and winked and hardly stopped winking; it seemed to lick the house. And the thunder hardly stopped thundering; sometimes it rolled and grumbled, and sometimes it burst the air with a bang; but it, like the lightning, seemed to have singled out this house for its prey.

"Hey, Jule! Listen!" shouted Tom. He had to shout above the uproar. "Anyone could be coming into this house, any*thing* could be, and we'd never even hear it!"

But he was wrong. In one of those instants of lull, when the rain left to itself sounds peaceful and industrious, they heard something else—another sound—and it was in the house with them, yes, in this very house: hard, brisk footsteps, then an old voice calling . . .

"Uncle Pin?" breathed Tom, moving closer to Julian.

"Oh no, it's not him," whispered Julian, icy with the thought of Chinese ghosts.

"Listen—listen! Something is coming up the stairs!"

Something was. Something was coming, clicking and clattering—what? Oh, what? And then the sound was lost as the thunder burst itself apart, and burst the lightning with it. The world seemed to blow up.

Almost immediately there was a hideous tearing noise; a mighty crash *inside* the house!

And something white flashed by the door . . .

All this took only an instant, but when there is terror, an instant seems pinned motionless on time. The boys were clinging to each other, unashamed.

"The house has been struck," croaked Tom. "There'll be a fire."

"But the white thing! The white thing . . ."

There was another lull; in that last burst the storm seemed to have spent itself. Only the rain poured down and down; and now, quite close to them, the thin old voice called out again.

"Ma-a-a-a," it called.

Julian let go of Tom.

"It's only Uncle Sam! That crazy goat! He must have broken out of his pen."

"And come in here for shelter, I guess."

"Why here, I wonder? Why not somewhere else?"

But they would never know the reason. When they called him, Uncle Sam came clicking into the room, smelling strongly of wet goat, and the boys were so relieved, so glad to see him, that they gave him a chocolate bar to eat, paper and all.

"That crash though, brother, what was that?" Tom wondered, and sneezed. The air seemed suddenly thick and itchy. "Do you think we were struck?"

"No," said Julian, ashamed that his teeth were chattering still. "I think—I think that Uncle Sam finished off the s-stairs."

And that is what had happened, as they saw when they went to investigate. They could see, by the diminishing, fitful lightning, that where the stairs had been there was a chasm, edged with a hanging fringe of balustrade. The stifling cloud of dust and wood particles was beginning to settle now, but the boys kept sneezing.

"How'll we ever get down from here, I wonder?" said Tom.

"There are back stairs. Bound to be," Julian assured him.

"We'll have to wait till daylight to find them. We'd never do it in the dark; the floor back there is full of holes. I'm sorry, Jule, but I certainly think it was a *crazy* idea not to bring a flashlight. I certainly think it was *dumb*."

"So I agree with you now," Julian admitted handsomely. "It was idiotic and it was stupid and it was asinine. There. That satisfy you?"

"Sure. I guess so. Anyway, we've still got something to eat. That's one good thing."

They had another snack in the pitch dark, and Uncle Sam was glad to share it with them, but it caused Julian to remember about being thirsty.

The thunder had rolled itself away; the lightning was gone; but luckily the rain was heavy. It poured in a stream from the broken gutter above the window.

"Hold me by the belt, Tom, will you, and don't let me fall out? If I don't get a drink, I'll die."

So Tom gripped the back of Julian's belt, and Julian, by leaning far out of the window and practically dislocating his neck, was able to get his mouth into position under the spout and gulp down rainwater. It tasted of rust and wood and creosote and

dead leaves and sparrows, but the main thing was that it was *wet*.

After he had drunk all he could, he held onto Tom's belt and performed the same service for him. Then they ate the last of the peanuts to take the taste of the rainwater out of their mouths, and after that they rolled themselves up in their blankets—it was cooler now—and lay down in the darkness.

"I'll never forget this night, man," Tom said. "Wait till we tell the kids: a real live ghost story."

"A real live goat story, you mean, and Uncle Sam's not the only goat," said Julian with a weary yawn. "I don't think anything makes you so tired as being good and scared and then getting over it."

Soon, in spite of their hard bed, they were sound asleep. The rain poured steadily all night. Uncle Sam settled down beside them for a while, but toward morning he wandered into the hall and began nibbling at the tatters of wallpaper that hung loose from the wall. He nibbled thoughtfully and rather daintily like someone eating celery at a dinner party.

14

Advice to Librans

"Well, I think it's disgusting, perfectly *disgusting*, of them to have gone off without us that way, without telling us or anything," Portia said to Lucy, and Lucy agreed.

"Boys think they're the only ones who are entitled to adventure," she said. "I bet we would have been just as brave as they were."

"Braver!" declared Portia, and she stayed mad at Julian for two whole days.

Because of course the story of the boys' escapade had come out almost immediately.

In the first place they had overslept that morning. When they woke up, it was broad daylight; the rain was gone and the sun was out; Uncle Sam was clicking restlessly about the room.

"Jumping cats, it's almost nine o'clock!" Tom yelped. "I'll be late to the store and Mr. Bilmeyer will bawl me out!"

"I'll be late with my newspapers, and *everyone* will bawl me out!" said Julian. Hastily they bundled their belongings together and made for the back stairs, Uncle Sam following.

The only trouble was that there were no back stairs. They apparently had collapsed or been hacked away by vandals years ago.

"There might be a tree by a window, or something," Tom offered hopefully. "We could get down that way."

But there was no tree that grew near enough; and to jump was out of the question.

"All we can do is yell," Julian said; so they leaned out of a window on the north side of the house and bellowed till they were hoarse.

"Uncle Pi-in! Oh, Uncle *Pi-in!*"

But there was no sign of him, and it was getting later by the minute, so they went to a window on the south side of the house and bellowed there.

"Aunt Minneha-ha! Aunt Minneha-*haaa!*" they bawled.

And she, luckily, did hear them. She came out of her house, Tarrigo barking beside her, and glanced to and fro, searching for the source of the yells.

"Up here, Aunt Minnehaha, up here in Judge Chater's house!"

Mrs. Cheever settled her spectacles on her nose and peered up at them.

"So *that's* where you are! Well, I declare! Your parents are worried to death, boys, and my brother has gone off in the Machine to search for you. You had better come down at once!"

"But we *can't,* Aunt Minnehaha!" And they explained the matter to her.

"Ma-a-a-a!" contributed Uncle Sam, as he joined them at the window and looked out, with his beard draped over the sill.

"Meet our roommate," Tom said, and Mrs. Cheever laughed and laughed.

"So that's where *he* is. My brother will be relieved to know—and here he comes right now, thank fortune!"

But then, as luck would have it, Mr. Payton had no ladder tall enough—Judge Chater's taste had run to lofty ceilings—so Mr. Caduggan had to be fetched with his. And even after the boys were safely on the ground, poor Uncle Sam remained aloft, bleating wistfully, for though goats are very good at climbing cliffs, they are very poor at climbing ladders, particularly *down.*

In the end, Mr. Caduggan had to improvise a sort of hammock and, with the aid of a couple of friends, got Uncle Sam into the thing and lowered him from a window. One of the friends, who had thoughtfully brought a camera along, took a picture of the majestic descent and turned it over to the

Pork Ferry Sentinel, which printed it, subsequently, with a complete account of the situation.

So that any element of secrecy for which the boys had hoped lay shattered in a thousand pieces.

"You can't get away with anything in this life," Julian remarked gloomily. "At least *I* can't."

He and Tom had been roundly scolded: by their parents, by their employers, by the girls. The little boys, however, showed the proper perspective and regarded them as heroes. And Joe was deeply envious.

"Here I just simply went to bed, just for a little catnap, all dressed and everything," he told them. "I even took the alarm clock with me to make certain. I stuffed it in between two pillows, right under my ear (because I didn't want my folks to know, *you* know), and then what did I do! When the doggone clock went off, I just reached in and shut it off! In my *sleep* I mean! How about that! To think you can double-cross yourself like that, in your own sleep!"

"I think I'll stay mad at them another day," Portia said. "It's getting hard to do it; I keep forgetting, but I'm going to try."

"All right, then I will, too," Lucy said cheerfully. "Madame Vavasour says Librans are apt to be too kind-hearted for their own good."

She and Portia had been consulting, as they

often did, *Mme. Vavasour's Gypsy-Witch Fortune Teller*; a useful volume they had found in Mrs. Brace-Gideon's library. The only parts they really read were those concerning people born under the sign of Libra, as Portia and Lucy both had been, within a week of one another, early in October.

"You are inordinately fond of luxury," Madame Vavasour had informed them. "All the appointments and appurtenances of the *haut monde*"—Lucy had some trouble reading *haut monde* out loud, but it didn't matter—"are to you as the glowing candle-flame is to the fluttering moth. Visits to elegant spas and watering places, luxurious railroad travel, fine horses, fine wines and impeccable *cuisine*, are hardly less than necessities to one of your elegant and pleasure-loving tastes. If you are a member of the fair sex, you will concern yourself with naught but the most exquisite gems, the finest furs, the hand-somest members of the opposite sex—"

"The heck with the handsomest members of the opposite sex," Portia had interrupted. "What I like is the part about fine horses and luxurious railroad travel."

"Well, I don't mind about the exquisite gems and finest furs," Lucy confessed, giving herself a sideways glance in the mirror. She was fairly sure she was going to be pretty when she grew up; in fact, she thought she might be starting to be already.

However, they knew that section of the *Gypsy-Witch Fortune Teller* by heart, so they skipped it today and went on to the section called: "The Inner Sanctum: Mme. Vavasour's Incomparable and Invaluable Compendium of Mystic Insights. Supernaturally-Directed Counsels on Matters of Health, Money, and the Heart; also a Definitive Listing of the True Meaning and Prophecies of Dreams."

"Wow!" Lucy said the first time she read it. "And look; she's got twelve pages, a page for each month, for every single sign of the Zodiac. They tell you what to expect and what to do about it and all."

"Now how could she know, though," Portia had objected. "I mean how could she know about *now?* The book came out in 1889, for goodness' sake!"

"I don't know. She probably had some sort of secret power or something: after all she was right about our characters, wasn't she? Luxury-loving and generous and kindhearted, and all. You know that's the way we are, Portia, even if some people don't realize it."

"Well, I guess so. I hope so," Portia said a little dubiously. She was the one who had the book today—they were very strict about taking turns—and as she riffled through the pages, she was stopped for a moment by the Dream section. She usually was.

"Listen; did you know that if you dream about

darning socks, it means you're going to find money in the street?"

"No. And I don't think that's very useful information; how can you make yourself dream about darning socks? I never dreamed about that in my whole life."

"I don't think I ever did, either. Well, here we are: 'Advice to Librans for the Month of August.' "

Portia began to read aloud. August, in Madame Vavasour's point of view, was rather a poor month for Librans. Caution was the keynote. They would have to be careful all month long; careful of their health, of their possessions, careful about accidents, suspicious of Good Offices proffered by any but their Nearest and Dearest, and constantly on the lookout for Traducers—"Whatever they are," Lucy said.

"Traitors, probably, like Julian and Tom and Joe," was Portia's opinion.

Above all, Librans were to be careful about money and valuables. They could not be too careful, and were to Lie Low. "This month will not be profitable or eventful to those of you born under the Sign of the Scales," Madame Vavasour concluded. "Expect little in the way of pleasure or enrichment. It will be vexing, nay, onerous to you who so highly value the Good Things of Life; but attempt to accept this period of retrenchment with Patience and Humility.

Wait and Hope, and guard with care those valuables already in your possession."

Portia threw the book down.

"What valuables; my tooth braces?" she demanded sarcastically. "Lucy, I wish we'd never read it. Now we have nothing to look forward to but being bored!"

"Oh, pooh, I don't believe a word of it. I don't *really* believe she had any secret power. Neither do you. I think she was just writing about some dead old boring August in eighteen-eighty-whatever-it-was."

"Do you really?"

"I really do. But I still think she was very good about character," Lucy said . . .

The girls were sitting on the window seat in Portia's room with the door closed. It was a dull, gray day, and Foster and Davey had thunderously invaded the house, bringing with them a fresh supply of boys their own age. They seemed to be doing an extraordinary amount of shouting and pounding up and downstairs.

"Boys just have to be noisy," Lucy observed critically. "They just naturally have to be noisy, the way a chicken has to have feathers. I don't know why."

"Daddy always says what Mark Twain said about

them—you know, the Tom Sawyer man—*he* said that what a small boy is, is a 'loud noise with dirt on it'. . . . Listen to Gulliver, too, but of course he can't help it; he's a boy himself."

"They should take lessons from Mousenick," Lucy said, stroking the tiny cat, asleep beside her. "Wouldn't it be nice if we could keep him a kitten forever?"

"I wish we could." Portia stood up, stretching and yawning. "And I wish there was something to *do*."

There seemed to be nothing whatever to do. It was that sort of day. The big boys had gone off somewhere; but of course it didn't matter to her because she and Lucy were mad at *them*; and the little boys were busily unraveling peace inside the house. . . . Portia wandered over to the mirror and looked at herself.

"And I wish I didn't have these *freckles*," she complained.

"It is too bad." Lucy agreed wholeheartedly. "Isn't there a cure for them? Some kind of cold cream or something? Listen; what about that stuff of Mrs. Brace-Gideon's: that Princess Something-or-other's Elixir of whatcha-macallit that was supposed to give you a 'pearly complexion'? Has your mother thrown it away?"

"Why no, I don't think so, yet. But she will any minute because Mr. Horton's about ready to paint the bathroom, finally. Why, that's a good idea, Lucy, and if the stuff is all dried up, we'll just add water to it. Maybe after all these years it will be stronger, too . . ."

At this moment the door of Portia's room burst open, and small boys came flooding in, wearing Indian war bonnets and whooping like yahoos.

"I'm Big Chief Fang!" Foster shouted happily. "We've come to scalp you! We've come to *tomahawk* you and *scalp* you!"

"No, you have not! You get right out of my room!" commanded Portia, giving him a whack with the *Gypsy-Witch Fortune Teller*. She and Lucy, being older, larger, and more impressive, were able to sweep them out of the room and close the door.

"They won't stay out, though," Portia said, as she and Lucy leaned against the door and heard the scuffles and giggles going on outside. "We'll just have to make a break for the bathroom. It has a real lock on it, thank goodness."

They held the door fast a moment longer, then released it suddenly, leaping away as it flew open and the little tribe of aborigines came spilling in, in a tangle.

The girls sprinted down the hall, laughing and

lively now, leaped into the bathroom, and closed and locked the door, just in time.

"Heck, no fair," objected Big Chief Fang in the hall. "You're not supposed to use locks. Come on out!"

"Never!" sang Portia.

"Never, never, never!" sang Lucy.

"Oh, well, who cares! *Stay* in there then; stay all year. All you'll have to eat is withered-up old pills," said Big Chief Fang.

"Oig," said another Indian who sounded like Davey.

"Come on, you guys; let's go and ask my mother for a cooky," invited the Chief, and away they all thundered, down the hall and down the stairs.

"Peace at last," said Lucy. Then she caught a glimpse of herself in the mirror above the basin. "Heavens, is my skin really that color? *Green?*"

"Oh, no, it makes everybody look like that. But that's not where she kept her medicines. They're over here in this wall thing."

Portia tugged at the handle of the little cabinet door.

"You should have seen Jule searching for Mrs. Brace-Gideon's safe in here. In a *bath*room, imagine! *Honest*ly!"

"Honestly," echoed Lucy.

"Now, what's the matter with *this* door? The rainstorm's made everything stick all over again."

She gave the handle a mighty yank, and to her infinite amazement the whole cabinet swung forward; swung outward toward her from the wall like a heavy little door, which is exactly what it was.

And there behind it was the safe.

15

The Safe

Portia made one of those peculiar sounds that signify sudden and total astonishment: something between a gasp and a squeal.

"It's it!"

"Mrs. Brace-Gideon's real live safe!" Lucy whispered in awe.

"I don't believe it, though. I just simply can't believe it," Portia said.

"But it's real! My goodness, Portia, look at all those numbers and little metal doorknobs. Why, it's the realest-looking thing I ever saw!"

Portia gave a leap. "Come *on*, then, we must tell Mother. . . . *Mother*, oh MOTHER!" shouted Portia, flinging the door open, storming along the hall and down the stairs.

"Mo—*ther!!*"

"Portia, for heaven's sake!" exclaimed Mrs. Blake, emerging from the kitchen. "You sound like a trumpeting elephant! What in the world is the matter!"

"We've found the safe, Mother! We've finally found it!"

"You've found the what?" said Mrs. Blake, utterly confused.

"Oh *Mother*, the *safe*! Mrs. Brace-Gideon's wall safe! The thing she kept her money in; *you* know."

"Her safe? Really? Are you sure?" said Mrs. Blake.

"Oh, *M*other," Portia repeated impatiently. "Come and see for your own self!" She took her mother's hand and pulled her, hurried her, to the stairs.

"It's really true, Mrs. Blake, it really is, it's really true," Lucy kept babbling, right at their heels as they ran up the steps. And right at her heels came the members of the Indian band, with their mouths full of cooky.

"In the *bath*room?" expostulated Mrs. Blake. "How could it possibly be in the b—" But by then they had ushered her in, and she saw what they had seen: the medicine cabinet swung out from the wall, and in the wall the little metal door with its nickel knobs and dials, the little door that had been hidden all these years!

"Why, I never—I absolutely never—" murmured Mrs. Blake, almost at a loss for words. Then she said: "How do you suppose we'll get it open?"

Portia gave another of her leaps.

"Julian!" she exclaimed. "Jule has the combination, Mother; he found it in the helmet!"

"He found it *where?*" begged poor Mrs. Blake, but nobody was there to tell her; already they were tumbling and galumphing down the stairs.

The big front door flew open and stayed open. The children, led by Portia, streamed across the lawn.

"Jul—i—an! Oh, *Jule!*" roared Portia, marveling even as she did so at her own lung power.

But the big boys were nowhere to be seen; nowhere within earshot, either, obviously.

"They must have gone to Gone-Away; where else *would* they go?" suggested Lucy.

So off they all went, jog-trotting along the wooded drive; Portia first, her tooth braces blinking and her bangs standing straight up in the wind; Lucy next, with her curls bouncing; and chugging along behind them came the Indian braves, still eating as they ran.

As it happened, Julian and Tom and Joe had spent the afternoon at Gone-Away, helping Mr. Payton build a stronger goatpen for the vagrant Uncle Sam.

It was always interesting to build things at Gone-Away, because no new material was ever used; it was necessary to improvise, and this in itself was a challenge.

The goatpen in the first place had been an ingenious barricade contrived of chicken wire, old doors, old bedsprings. And today the boys and Mr. Payton had reinforced it with more doors, more bedsprings, and a length of railing from the Delaneys' fallen porch. They had also added a wrought-iron gate from somebody's forgotten driveway; and that gave it a touch of elegance.

"Ma-a-a-a," said Uncle Sam, sounding perfectly disgusted. He stood on his hind legs and stared at them balefully through the wrought-iron gate.

"Yes indeed, sir, yes indeed," Mr. Payton replied to him. "This will keep you in your place for a while. Until the next time. For there will be a next time, I'll be bound," he added to the boys. "Uncle Sam has the soul of a vagabond and the ingenuity of a born thief."

He removed his hat and blotted his forehead with a handkerchief.

"Let us go to my house and have a drink of water. Later my sister may have something better to offer."

For some reason Mr. Payton's kitchen pump seemed to produce the coldest, clearest water in the region, like the water of a mountain spring. Perhaps, Julian thought, it was because they usually drank it after they had been working hard or playing hard.

When the boys had had all they wanted, they

drifted into Mr. Payton's living room. It was very different from his sister's: barer. There were many books piled up in piers, but very little furniture. There were no pictures on the walls; only a piece of tacked-up wrapping paper with words printed on it, and none of them could read the words because they were written in Latin.

Joe and Tom sat on the horsehair sofa, looking blank and comfortably worn-out. Julian, on the floor, had propped his back against the bed, and Mr. Payton, bolt upright on one of his bolt upright little chairs, was lighting his pipe, coaxing it and coaxing it along.

Julian sighed contentedly. It's good to work hard, then to rest, he thought. His aimless eye caught sight again of the black letters painted on the wrapping paper.

"Uncle Pin, what is that Latin thing?" he asked. "What does it say? I've wondered for a long time, but I keep forgetting to ask."

Mr. Payton puff-puffed his pipe; it had come to life now, and he turned his head to look at the paper on the wall.

"The words are very old, Julian. They were written hundreds of years ago by a man who loved nature and who became a saint: Saint Francis of Assisi. It's sort of a hymn of praise. They call it a canticle: the canticle of the sun . . .

" 'Praised be my Lord with all his creatures,' it says, 'and especially our brother the sun who brings us the day and who brings us the light; fair is he, and shining with very great splendor: O Lord he signifies to us thee!

" 'Praised be my Lord for our sister the moon, and for the stars, which he has set clear and lovely in heaven.

" 'Praised be my Lord for our brother the wind, and for air and cloud, calms and all weathers, by which thou upholdest in life all creatures.

" 'Praised be my Lord for our sister water, who is very serviceable unto us, and humble and precious and clean.

" 'Praised be my Lord for our brother fire, through whom thou givest his light in the darkness; and he is bright and pleasant, and very mighty and strong . . .' "

Mr. Payton read on in his calm quiet voice till he came to the end of the canticle.

"I like that part about brothers and sisters," Tom said. "The sun *would* be a brother, and the moon *would* be a sister . . ."

Nobody else said anything. Fatly had come to settle by Julian's leg. He had turned on his purr at middle register; not his loudest purr. Still, they could hear it.

And then they heard something else.

"Julian! Oh, *Ju*—ule!"

Julian sighed and stood up.

"Girls," he remarked, and went to the door. He opened it wide and leaned out. "Here we are, Porsh," he called, "here at Uncle Pin's."

Portia and Lucy and the Indians blew breathless into the house.

"We've found it, Jule." Portia panted. "We've found the safe!"

"The safe? You mean the *safe?*"

"Mrs. Brace-Gideon's!" contributed Lucy.

"Oh, *brother!*" Julian shouted. "But I have to go home to get the paper with the combination on it. I'll hurry back—I've got my bike—and I'll meet you at your house—" Halfway through the door he turned back. "*Where* did you find it, though?"

When Portia told him he said, "See? What did I say?" Then he vanished.

"You come with us, Uncle Pin," Portia said. "And let's get Aunt Minnehaha, too. We should all be there together when he opens it."

Julian, on reaching home, leaped from his bike, allowing it to fall, leaped into the house, shouting the news to his mother, and attained his room without having touched the stairs; or so it seemed.

There followed a few minutes of panic because he could not remember what he had done with the slip. Collections of birds' nests and seashells were toppled about, drawers were pulled out and their contents clawed into a muddle, the pockets of his coats and trousers were searched; and then, of course, he found the slip exactly where he had put it: in plain sight, on his worktable, with a fossil stone to hold it down.

"I'll drive you back, Julian," his mother said. "It will save time, and besides, I wouldn't miss this event for anything!"

It was a peculiar gathering to assemble in anybody's bathroom: two pretty women, five biggish children, assorted; five smallish ones, boys, wearing war feathers; one elderly lady dressed in the fashion of the Gay Nineties; one elderly gentleman with a distinguished beard and clothes not much more recent. Also two dogs and one small kitten. Though the room was large, it wasn't really large enough. The Indians obligingly removed their shoes and stood in the bathtub.

"Now," said Julian.

They waited breathlessly.

Julian carefully wiped his fingers with a handkerchief. (He had seen someone do this on TV.) Then he lightly touched the T-shaped hand on the dial. He looked as though he had been doing this sort of thing all his life.

"Now it's on zero, see?" He said. "That's where

it has to be first. So. Here we go. Six turns to the right. One . . . two . . . three . . . four . . . five . . . six. There, I heard the tumblers fall. Now two turns to the left. One . . . two . . ."

Slowly, meticulously, he followed exactly the instructions on the slip of paper. At the last, after the "three whole turns R to eight," he paused dramatically.

"Want me to go on?"

"Oh, hurry up! Hurry up!"

Julian grinned, put out his hand, and opened the small heavy door. Inside the safe there was still another little door with a key in its lock. Above, and on either side, the shelves and pigeonholes were empty.

"Turn the key! Turn the key!"

So Julian turned the key and opened the door to the interior cupboard of the safe. Everyone pressed forward in a bunch. And then there was a sort of collective groan in the room because that little cupboard, like Mother Hubbard's famous one, was bare; bare even of dust.

"Well, I didn't think there'd be anything in it. I never did," said Portia, disappointed to be right.

"But what about that little drawer *under* the door?" Lucy asked.

"I can't get it open. It's locked and the key's gone."

"Try the one in the cupboard door . . ."

But the key didn't fit.

"Perhaps I can force it," Mr. Payton said, coming forward. "Since returning to Gone-Away, I have become fairly expert at breaking locks. Had to. Couldn't get into the Big House any other way." He turned to Mrs. Blake. "With your permission?"

"But of course, of course!"

With the head of his heavy walking stick Mr. Payton dealt the lock a number of sharp blows.

"I think perhaps now . . . but I need something to pull it open with. There is no handle."

Foster, with great presence of mind, stepped out of the bathtub and handed Mr. Payton Baron Bloodshed's buttonhook, which had been spending the summer in his pocket with other curious items.

"Maybe this'll do."

"Ah, excellent, Foster, thank you. Yes, yes indeed. . . . Look!"

Mr. Payton pulled open the little drawer, which was lined with blue plush and filled with small labeled packets.

Hands reached out; Foster's grubby ones among them.

"No, wait a bit, wait a bit," Mr. Payton commanded. "I think the privilege should go to Mrs. Blake."

But Mrs. Blake said: "I think it should go to

Lucy and Portia. They're the ones who found the safe."

Portia's fingers were shaking when she lifted the first packet out and read the label: "Mamma's Garnet Parure."

"What's a parure?" said Foster.

It turned out to be a set of jewelry: a garnet necklace with earrings and brooch to match, sparkling and dark and clear as wine.

"How *beautiful!*"

"Mine says: 'Great-Aunt Sophronisba's Brooch with Uncle Walter's Hair'!" Lucy announced.

This turned out to be a large gold-framed pin enclosing a small fine-woven mat of dark brown hair!

"Oh, yes, hair jewelry was much the fashion in my grandmother's day," Mrs. Cheever said.

"Did they ever use teeth?" Foster wanted to know, thinking of his own old front ones, but Mrs. Cheever said she thought not.

The girls in greatest excitement went on opening the little packets. Mrs. Cheever, Mrs. Blake, and Aunt Hilda hovered about them, fascinated. Mr. Payton was interested, too. But the boys were rather disappointed; jewelry didn't mean much to them.

"Here's 'Great-Grandfather Dadware's Signet Ring'!" said Portia, holding up a massive ring with a carnelian intaglio set in gold.

"And here are 'Great-Grandmother Dadware's

Cameo Bracelets,' " said Lucy, displaying the lovely things: circlets of ovals, and on each oval a little face was exquisitely carved.

There were necklaces of paste and pinchbeck and jet and amber; there were gold earrings and silver ones, and ones made out of coral and of turquoise. There were bracelets woven of gold wire, and many brooches, and fine-link chains and lockets of gold and onyx. There were seed pearls all gone black with age, and cold jade beads from which the silken cord had rotted away. Many of the things were beautiful, and some were ruined. All were very old.

The last packet contained the prettiest thing of all. "Great-great Grandmother's Betrothal Ring." It looked like a cobweb heavy-set with dew.

"Rose diamonds!" Aunt Hilda said. "Barbara, it can't be later than the eighteenth century, and probably it's older!"

"Then I suppose these things were left behind in the safe just as the furniture was left in the attic," Mrs. Blake speculated. "Partly because they were too good to throw away; partly because of family sentiment. And none of them to Mrs. Brace-Gideon's own personal taste."

"Oh, no indeed! Indeed they would not have been," Mrs. Cheever asserted. "They would never have been costly enough. Or showy enough. When

it came to jewelry, Mrs. Brace-Gideon inclined toward the flamboyant, didn't she, Pin?"

"Had a diamond that looked like a hotel doorknob," Mr. Payton said. "I remember it well."

"And that emerald I told you about. And rubies;
great clumps and clots of rubies all mobbed together;
and a pin, a gold pin shaped like an eagle, with
ruby eyes; and a water-lily pin as big as my hand,
made out of opals. . . . Oh, no, these never would
have suited her!"

"Thank fortune," Mrs. Blake said, as she had
said so often this summer.

The girls, dripping with jewels, were delighted
with all that they had found.

"Well, I'll tell you one thing, Portia," Lucy said.
"I'll never believe another word of Madame Vavasour's, not even about our characters. This has been
the most exciting day I've ever spent!"

"I know. Just look at all these lovely things.
What could be more wonderful to find?"

"Money," Foster answered promptly. "I wish it
had been some old-time money. Or an old-time gun,
or two guns, or some skulls and bones, or something
*in*teresting!"

16

A New Old Name

Every Friday evening when Mr. Blake returned to spend the weekend, the first thing he did was to take a "tour of inspection," both inside the house and outside. Every new thing was of interest: every flower, every shrub, every pair of curtains or new coat of paint. The safe with its little cache of jewels had fascinated him, and now and then, just to feel splendid, he wore Captain Dadware's signet ring.

Now, on a Friday late in August, he was strolling on the lawn, arm in arm with Mrs. Blake. Portia had his other arm, and Foster was dawdling along beside, before, or behind them, as the mood took him. But he stayed near. Gulliver had performed his leaping dance of welcome, and now was strolling about, too, sniffing for rabbits. Mousenick, composed and quiet, was sitting on the doormat, waiting to feel playful again.

"You know, it's really turning into a handsome house," Mr. Blake said. "Well, not handsome, perhaps, but distinguished. Substantial. Interesting."

"I think it's just beautiful," Portia said, and her mother agreed with her.

They all stood looking up at their house with satisfaction. It was warmed by the late afternoon sunshine, and in the rich ivy, here and there showing a ruddy leaf already, sparrows were rustling and squabbling.

"But I don't really mind them, do you?" Mrs. Blake said. "I've never minded sparrows as much as you're supposed to. . . ." They began strolling on again. "Oh, Paul, did I tell you what Aunt Minnehaha told me? No, I didn't. She only told me yesterday. She says that this house was built on the site of another one, a very grand one that was built more than two hundred years ago. But then about 1830 it was struck by lightning and burned to the ground . . ."

"Amberside," said Foster, walking beside her.

"Hmm? What did you say, darling?" asked his mother, smoothing down his cowlick as she liked to do.

"Amberside. That was the house's name. The other house's. The one that burned."

"Was it really? How do you know?"

"That's what Eli Scaynes says. He says his grandma told him so, and her grandma told her."

"Amberside . . . Amberside . . ."

"You never told me that, Foster." Portia reproached him.

"You never asked me," Foster replied reasonably. "I knew it a long time. I knew it the first day Eli came to work here. He told me when he was riding me around in his wheelbarrel."

"Amberside," Mrs. Blake repeated thoughtfully, stopping to look at the house again, looking at it with her head on one side and her eyes narrowed.

"It would be a good name to give to one of those yellow cats," Portia observed.

"It would be a good name to give to a house, too," her father said.

"Yes, it would," Mrs. Blake agreed. "Oh, it would, Paul, wouldn't it? It suits it; now, anyway, with the late sun on it like this . . . and later, in September, when the maples are pure yellow . . .

"And later still on winter nights with all the windows lighted . . ."

"Winter nights! We'll never see it on winter nights," said Portia sadly.

"Perhaps you will . . ."

"Oh, tell them, Paul, do tell them! I can't keep the secret one more minute!"

"What secret?" Portia demanded, already joy-fully suspecting.

"What secret, Daddy?" cried Foster, jumping. Gulliver barked.

"How would you like to live here all year round?" asked their father.

How would they like it! The mere thought made them jerk and prance and squeal!

"Because I think I'm going to work on the paper with Uncle Jake and write my book on the side. So that would mean we'd have to live here all the time."

"And I could go to school at Julian's school!" cried Portia.

"And I could go to school at Davey's!" cried Foster.

"And we'd learn how to ski—"

"And ice-skate and wear snowshoes."

"And go to see Aunt Minnehaha and Uncle Pin all winter long!"

"And Gulliver would like it so much better," said Foster, sounding a virtuous, unselfish note.

"Of course we'll have to put heat in the house and pretty soon at that," Mr. Blake said. "Probably electricity, too."

"There goes the Hepplewhite breakfront," Mrs. Blake remarked cryptically. "But it's worth it."

"Oh, *wait* till I tell Julian!" And off went Portia in one of her great swooping dances of delight.

"Amberside," Mrs. Blake said to Mr. Blake. "Amberside the second; but we'll leave off 'the second.' Doesn't it sound nice, though? 'Mr. and Mrs. Paul Bannister Blake who live at Amberside with their daughter and their son and their dog and their cat'!"

So at last the new old house had a new old name to be called by. Mr. Blake painted the name on a signpost to stand at the entrance of the drive; and Mrs. Blake had it printed at the top of all the letter paper and on the flaps of all the envelopes.

Gradually people began to speak of the place as Amberside, though there were a few diehards who never stopped calling it the Villa Caprice, or, as in the case of Eli Scaynes, the Villa *Cay*-priss.

But Julian and Joe and Tom and Lucy and Davey never called it anything except "the Blakes's house"; and Portia and Foster never called it anything but "home." All their lives they knew that one of the best things that ever happened to them was to be able to call it that.

Elizabeth Enright (1909–1968) grew up in New York in a family of artists. She spent her childhood drawing pictures and created both art and story for her first book, *Kintu: A Congo Adventure*, published in 1935. She later decided that she preferred writing to illustrating and went on to write many enduringly popular books, including a series about the Melendy family in *The Saturdays* and three other novels; and two long fairy tales, *Tatsinda* and *Zeee*. She won numerous awards, including the Newbery Medal for *Thimble Summer* (1938) and a Newbery Honor for *Gone-Away Lake* (1957).